THE O'MA... ...T CRIME
T... ...ERS

FOXTON GIRLS

Copyright © 2021 by K.T. Galloway

Published worldwide by A.W.E. Publishing.

This edition published in 2021

Edited by Beverley Sanford

Cover design by Meg Jolly

www.ktgallowaybooks.com

FOXTON GIRLS

AN O'MALLEY & SWIFT NOVEL

K.T. GALLOWAY

To Gran B, thank you for passing down your cheeky sense of humour.

And to Gran and Grandad S, thank you for my love of all things horror!

BLURB

Their secrets die with them.

When a spate of suicides occur at prestigious girls' school, Foxton's, Psychotherapist Annie O'Malley is called in to talk with the students.

What Annie finds are troubled young girls full of secrets and lies; and a teacher caught in the midst.

Back working with DI Joe Swift, can Annie and Swift unravel the secrets together before it's too late?

The second in the Annie O'Malley Thrillers sees Annie facing her greatest challenge yet.

PROLOGUE

Florence's gaze flitted between the bedside clock and the man beside her. She loved him, she'd decided, not that it really mattered anymore as in precisely twelve minutes she would be dead.

She thought she may as well make the most of the time she had left. Flipping over on to her stomach, Florence let her hand trace a path over the scars on the man's naked torso. She felt him shiver and wake.

"You're still here? What time is it?" he said, his voice thick with sleep.

"Ten to," Florence replied.

Ten minutes.

She stretched her arms out and tried to roll on top of him. He pushed her away gently and eased himself up on to his elbows. The bed creaked under the shifting weight of his body.

"Go home."

Eight minutes.

The man dropped his legs out of the covers and perched on the edge of the bed; his head held in his hands, palms covering his eyes. His nails were bitten to the quick, the skin at the edges rough and red, peeling away from their flattened nail plates. After a moment he stood. He made his way in the dark to the door, a sliver of light peeking in under the threshold illuminated the floor by his feet. More scars twinkled white against his skin. The light flooded the room as he opened the door.

"Please, Florence. Go home."

Four minutes.

Florence gathered up her clothes and slipped into them without a word.

One minute.

She stepped out of the dark room and didn't look back.

Midnight.

FLORENCE BARELY NOTICED THE LOUD CHIRRUPING from her phone as she ran down the stairs of the small cottage. Sure footed with practice she reached the bottom before taking it out of her pocket and checking. Heart pounding, she looked down at the illuminated screen. Midnight exactly. The message was right on cue.

It's past your curfew. Get home before I tell the headmaster.

Pleasantly surprised at the lack of threat or swearing, Florence felt like the elastic band around her chest had snapped. She figured the sender was only in the early stages of drunkenness. Either that or she was typing with her left hand, unwilling to relinquish her glass long enough to type a more worthy message. Whichever it was, Florence stuck her middle finger up at her phone and pocketed it as quickly as she could. She was perhaps less dead than she had been fearing. She hoped when she got home the wrath wouldn't descend upon her in all its glory; even at seventeen it still scared her.

She stood still for a moment as her heart rate returned to resting. The bedroom floor creaked above her head and she heard the door slide open, so she tiptoed quickly to the hallway and found her boots by the front door. The air outside was crisp with the first October frost. Florence's breath clouded in front of her with the stark change in temperature from the warmth of the thick-walled old cottage with its real fire and knitted blankets.

She took the long way back, walking along a small footpath that led through woods choked with oaks and sycamores, the leaves starting to turn golden and red around their edges. Bramble bushes lined the pathway, threatening to catch at Florence's feet and legs. Without a falter in her step, Florence's hand reached out and stroked the tree where Emily was found hanging by her neck. She whispered a few words as she passed: not stopping, not looking. Florence felt her skin raise with goose bumps, a cold shiver ran up her neck and into her scalp like icy fingers stroking away under her thick auburn hair. Florence kept her eyes ahead, not looking back. She knew if she turned, she would see Emily swinging slowly in the night just as she had been when they'd found her. Instead, Florence quickened her pace forwards.

The night was illuminated by a full moon, but the canopy of trees kept the path under a blanket of darkness. Luckily, Florence knew the route well. She came to the front of the large stately building she called home in less than twelve minutes. There would be no point climbing the stone stairs to the ornately carved heavy front door as it would be locked up tight, protecting all those who lay beyond it. Instead, Florence crept around the side to one of the service doors and lifted the latch. With the door closed behind her she slipped out of her shoes and tiptoed silently down a servant's corridor. Florence lived in the west wing of the old Georgian building which, for the last hundred years, was home to Foxton's School for Girls.

The school was still and quiet, the lights out. A smile threatened to lift Florence's cheeks as she snuck past the closed doors to her left and right. A little further on was the kitchen, the door slightly ajar, a woman could be seen slumped over the island sound asleep, drink still in hand. Florence thought she looked like the stereotypical American mum; coiffed fake blonde hair, hourglass figure, pinny wrapped around her dress. Except this was rural Norfolk, sunny England, and this was real life, which was anything *but* stereotypical.

Just past the door to the kitchen were the stairs. Almost grinning now, Florence climbed them, looking forward to getting into her own bed safe and sound and free from a thrashing. Perhaps tonight she wouldn't be dead at all.

"Good evening, Miss Haversham."

Florence recognised the quietly powerful voice of her head teacher and screwed up her face, inches away from her door and her bed. She turned to face the man who towered over her.

"Hi, Dad," she whispered.

ONE

DAY ONE

ANNIE BUMPED THE DOOR OPEN WITH HER HIP AND entered the office to a small cheer. It would have boosted her confidence, but she was not oblivious that the cheer was, in fact, for the tray of Starbucks that was wobbling precariously on the tips of her fingers.

"O'Malley," Detective Inspector Joe Swift said, grabbing the tray before it toppled to the floor. "Has anyone ever told you what an asset you are to this team?"

He gave Annie a wink and started dishing out the drinks to the rest of the officers in the small team that made up their county branch of the Major Crime Unit. The four of them, Annie O'Malley, DI Joe Swift, DS Annabelle Lock, and DC Tom Page, were the only ones in the large, open plan office that was normally a hub of activity. The officers from other teams were obviously not as eager to start before eight, then again, maybe the others hadn't been called in at the crack of dawn by their boss.

"You only ever call me in when you want something!" Annie replied, grabbing her own flat white and dropping her bag on a desk that she had earmarked as her own because she had been here more often than not recently, despite not being *actual* police.

The office quietened as they all sat down and sipped their drinks. DI Swift tapped away at his keyboard, letting out the occasional grunt and hammering at the keys.

"You know me!" he said eventually, swinging his screen around so Annie could see it and beckoning her over.

Annie slid her chair across the worn-out carpet tiles and stopped at Swift's side. His computer screen was emblazoned with the image of a large stately home. Happy looking girls in blazers and red and yellow striped ties held books in neat classrooms, they walked joyfully down wood panelled corridors, and smiled through safety goggles in an impressive looking lab. Foxton's School for Girls was written in bold, clean point at the bottom of the page. Unobtrusive, as though the reader should already know the name of the school, or they were in the wrong place.

"What's this?" Annie asked, nodding her head at the screen which now showed a photo of the older students in rather short, grey PE skirts, brandishing hockey sticks and perfect white smiles. She raised an eyebrow at Swift whose face lit up in a flush.

"Shut it, O'Malley," he said, clearing his throat and clicking on the link marked *students*.

Annie didn't push it. Even though she'd been

working in Swift's team for nearly three months now, ever since he'd brought her onboard to help find two young missing girls, Annie didn't know that much about Swift's personal life except that his wife vanished into thin air a couple of years ago. Making jokes about schoolgirls was probably a little low, especially at this time in the morning.

The page loaded and the first thing that caught Annie's eye was the scrolling red banner informing students to contact their House Parent or Head Girl if they felt the need to talk. It was all very officious.

"Local, posh, girls' school," Swift said once his cheeks had returned to a normal colour. "Foxton's. Been around as a building for hundreds of years. Converted to a school in the last century, and run by the current headteacher for about twelve, thirteen years. It's very prestigious, fees are astronomical."

Annie was waiting for the punchline. She knew places like this, knew that what lay inside the grand facade was glossy, primped, and untouchable. She patted her frizzy, dark red curls, unconsciously trying to flatten them. Parents didn't pay those fees for their girls to turn out like she had. Failed police officer, failed psychotherapist, failed daughter and sister.

"Right," Annie said, still non-the-wiser why she was at work so early. "And the reason the Guv called me in here for a meeting at eight was...?"

"Because he loves seeing your face!" Swift snorted, not unkindly.

Annie gave Swift a withering look, trying to hold back a smile herself. DCI Strickland, their Guv, had tried to recruit Annie back to the police force after she had helped to bring home the missing girls that summer. But Annie had tried being a uniformed officer ten years previously and had not made it past the training period, instead she'd retrained as a psychotherapist and worked in probation. So, DCI Strickland had decided to hire her as a consultant psychotherapist to Swift's small MCU team instead. They could call on her whenever they needed an extra pair of hands. This was only her second case, and she was apprehensive that DCI Strickland was just using her consultancy as a cover-up to bring her in as a dogsbody.

But Annie knew that DCI Strickland did *not* love seeing her face. Mainly because having to hire Annie as a consultant and not a PC was pushing his budgets in a direction he tried to avoid at all costs. Strickland also tried to avoid Annie at all costs now too, doubling back on himself whenever he saw her walking the corridors of the station.

"Swift, O'Malley." Strickland's voice boomed across the open plan office. "Here. Now!"

"Summoned," Annie whispered under her breath, giving Strickland a salute when his back was turned.

"O'Malley," Swift said, his eyes wide. "Some of us don't want to lose our jobs, thanks. Toe the line."

Strickland's office was tucked away in the far corner of the large open, plan room. Swift gave a rap at the door, rattling the glass, etched so visitors knew who they could find inside.

"Enter," Strickland boomed, and Annie snorted ironically.

"Chief," Swift said, pushing the door open and holding it for Annie.

"Guv," Annie said, full of professionalism.

The DCI's office was dark and inherently masculine. Grey walls and thick wooden furniture that looked like it had never been polished took up most of the small space. Annie had no idea how he found what he needed on his huge desk, or the desk itself, it was so hidden in paperwork.

"Sit," the man barked, as Swift shut the door and blocked out all the light.

Annie groped about in the darkness and felt her way to a chair, hoping she wasn't about to end up sitting in Swift's lap, or worse, Strickland's. As her eyes adjusted from the bright light of the main office she took in the Chief Inspector. Strickland always looked like he was one sausage roll away from a coronary, his pink face blended into his pink neck like a can of corned beef popping free from its tin and he needed to go up a few sizes in a collar that strained with every ragged breath he drew. Annie always found herself holding her own breath in his presence, as if this could delay the inevitable stroke.

"Foxton's," he said, more strained than normal. "Tell me what you know?"

Annie looked to Swift for this one.

"There's been a suicide," Swift said. "One of the sixth form."

Annie thought back to the happy looking hockey photo and wondered what had happened to cause one of those students to take her own life.

The DCI grunted.

"Why are we getting involved in a suicide, Chief?" Swift asked.

Strickland shuffled in his seat, the chair spinning from side to side as he tried to right himself.

"Evans noticed something weird in the pathology report," Strickland said, coughing, his face puce. "Go and see him when you're done here. But I'm reluctant to close the case and pass to the coroner until this has been sorted. Hopefully it's a case of dotting the t's and crossing the i's but until that's done, we treat this death as suspicious."

Dotting the t's? Annie bit her lip.

"Chief," Swift said, rising from his chair and pulling at his own collar.

It was hot in the DCI's office; a mix of testosterone and lack of windows made the air too thick to breathe. Strickland flung open a drawer in his desk, it rattled and stuck where paper jammed into the runners. With sausage fingers, Strickland flicked through the files and pulled one out. It was thin and yellow, and looked pretty nondescript.

"Emily Langton." Strickland handed the file over to Swift as a trickle of sweat dripped down his temple. "O'Malley, I want you in on this one to talk to the girls who knew Emily. Try and find out what was going on in her life, school life mainly. And talk to Emily's parents *only* and I mean only, if you absolutely have to."

"Chief," Annie said, eyeing the thin folder in Swift's hands.

She got up to leave too, the stench of coffee and masculine authority was making her stomach churn.

"And Swift, O'Malley?" Strickland looked ready to burst. "Whatever you do, keep this one on the down low. I do not want the press involved. I do not want the local community getting wind of what has happened. And I DO NOT want any gossip. Do you hear me?"

Annie stopped in her tracks, turning back to Strickland, as Swift pulled the office door open letting in a wash of cool air.

"Can I just ask why it's so important to keep this case so secret, Guv?" she asked, realising a bit too late that the purple tint on the tip of Strickland's nose was a sure sign that she probably *couldn't* ask.

"The headteacher, William Haversham, is a close and personal friend of mine," Strickland spluttered, as though Annie should already know this. "We play golf. Our wives drink together. It would be very embarrassing if he felt he couldn't trust *my* team."

Strickland put both hands on his desk and hauled himself up to his full height, towering over Annie despite her long legs.

"Now if you'll excuse me," he continued, his fingers turning white with the exertion of holding up his body weight. "I've got a meeting to get to."

Annie followed Swift out into the bright, coffee smelling open plan office, nearly getting whacked on the backside as Strickland slammed his door shut behind them.

"I think that went quite well," Annie said, smiling. "Don't you?"

TWO

THE MORGUE HAD NEVER BEEN ANNIE'S FAVOURITE place. Ever since she keeled over in her university dissection class when the lecturer had wheeled out not only a cadaver but also a tub of feet. That had been one in a comedy of errors in an undergraduate degree that Annie hadn't realised would involve dead bodies. She had only picked it for the psychology.

Silently cursing Evans, the pathologist, under her breath, Annie took out her phone and pretended to be engaged in something really important to take her mind off the dead teenager covered over on the gurney in the middle of the room. Even the smells as they'd pushed open the double doors and walked through the plastic flaps had old memories resurfacing, and Annie knew her breakfast wouldn't be too far behind. Luckily it had only been coffee!

"Didn't take you as squeamish," Swift said with a twinkle in his eye.

Annie gave him a withered look and went back to

Twitter and an argument she had stumbled upon about a recent celebrity encounter with the law. Just as she was getting to a juicy bit about said celebrity's unravelling sexual proclivities, Evans burst through the door with a folder in one hand and a half eaten Double Decker in the other. Soft nougat oozed from the centre and Annie swallowed furiously to try and dislodge the uncomfortable clod sitting in her throat. It didn't work.

"Swift," Evans boomed over the echoey morgue. "Good to see you again."

"I'd like to return the welcome, but, you know," Swift replied, nodding at the lump under the sheet.

"Of course, of course," Evans said, taking a bite of the chocolate bar and handing Swift the file before turning to look at Annie. "I don't think we've had the pleasure."

Annie winced when Evans held out his hand.

"It's okay," he laughed. "It's clean."

Annie flushed and felt like an idiot, taking his hand and shaking it.

"I'm Annie O'Malley," she said. "Psychotherapist."

"Ahh," Evans said, as if that explained her screwed up nose and altogether rather green pallor.

Evans shoved the last of his snack in his mouth and wiped away the crumbs from his lab coat. Annie had never met anyone like him. To look at he was a large brute of a man with a square chin and a shock of pink hair, and in any other situation, Annie would have crossed the road to avoid him. But he was actually a teddy bear, weirdly, given what he did for a living.

Swift moved closer to the trolley as Evans peeled gloves over his fingers and lifted the sheet covering Emily

Langton, folding it down delicately to her chest. She looked like she was asleep, her eyelids blue and fragile, her face pale. It was only the red welt of rope marks around her neck that gave away her cruel end.

Annie's breath stuttered and Swift was by her side in an instant, putting a hand on her shoulder.

"Are you sure you want to be here?" he whispered; all sense of his earlier mocking gone.

She nodded, not quite trusting herself to speak yet. This wasn't the first dead body she'd encountered out of the walls of the university dissection room, but there was something heart breaking about seeing a girl just about to start her life lying prone on a cold cutting table.

"Strickland said you had something for us?" Swift asked Evans, moving back to the trolley.

"Yup." Evans nodded to the file in Swift's hands. "It's all in there, but the gist of it is, Emily Langton had traces of Rohypnol in her blood."

"What?" Annie said, her stomach gaining a lining of steel with the revelation.

"Yeah." Evans nodded. He walked to an old looking computer in the corner and wiggled the mouse to fire it up. "Three hundred and fifty micrograms of Fluni-trazepam." He read. "Taken from a blood sample at least three hours after her death."

"What does that mean in layman's terms?" Annie asked as the two men exchanged knowing looks.

"That whoever gave Emily this drug wasn't just worried about retrograde amnesia," Swift answered, his eyebrows knitted together. "That's a lethal dose."

"So, she didn't die from hanging?" Annie said, shocked.

Evans came back to the trolley shaking his head.

"She did," he said. "Cause of death is still asphyxiation from complete hanging. But what we know now is that she would have been unconscious before she was up there."

"So, we're looking at homicide?" Swift said. "Why didn't the chief say that?"

"What *did* he say?" Evans was moving the sheet further down on Emily's body, and lifting out an arm.

"That you'd found something suspicious!" Swift replied.

"Hmm, that's what you get," Evans said. "He's bosom pals with the headteacher and I can't imagine either of them want the press associated with the homicide of a student, let alone a Foxton student!"

"Rohypnol's a date rape drug, isn't it?" Annie asked, trying not to imagine Strickland being bosom pals with anyone. "If she was drugged, were there any signs of sexual assault?"

"Weirdly," Evans said, holding up Emily's right arm. "There were signs of sexual activity at least a few hours prior to her death, but no signs of assault. It's almost impossible that Emily was under the influence of the Rohypnol when she was engaged in sexual activity either, as timescales would indicate she would have been dead from the overdose and not the hanging if that was the case."

Swift scratched his chin with his knuckles.

"So, let me get this straight," he said. "Emily had

probable consensual sex; she then took or was given a date rape drug, but not assaulted, then was strung up to hang. Why drug her after sex? Why hang her at all if she'd already been given a lethal dose?"

Annie was only half listening to the men talking. She'd noticed something on the arm of the murdered girl that Evans was holding up carefully in his huge hands.

"What's that?" she asked, edging as close as she dared.

"This," Evans said, turning the arm gently so the girl's palm was facing up. "You need to see."

Littered along the inside of her arm, the smooth, alabaster skin was punctured with red scratches. Annie looked even closer; the smell of the cleaning fluids itched her nostrils.

"Are they words?" she asked, taking a huge step back, her head spinning. "What on earth?"

"*Whoever keeps his mouth and his tongue keeps himself out of trouble.*" Evans put the arm gently back down and lifted the sheet back over Emily's face and head.

"What is that?" Swift asked.

"I ran it through the database, turns out it's a proverb, or a take on a proverb anyway."

"Did she do it herself?" Annie asked.

Evans shook his head. "The chief thought it might be her suicide letter to start with, made no great deal about it. In fact, he was pleased to see it because he thought it made the suicide nice and neat and tied up with a bow."

Swift muttered expletives under his breath and Evans gave him a wilted smile.

"Yep," the pathologist continued. "That was my first reaction too. But on further examination there was no way she could have done this to herself."

"Why?" Annie blurted.

"She after your job?" Evans asked Swift with a raised eyebrow.

"She's currently the best part of our team!" Swift said, and Annie couldn't tell if he was being facetious.

"Emily was right-handed." Evans addressed Annie now. "This was written on her right arm. Not only that, but there are also no half starts, no difference in the depth of the cuts. If you were doing this to yourself you would have at least a few attempts before you really went for it, no matter how suicidal you were feeling. And no-one would be able to cut themselves at such a deep level without panicking and stopping at points.

"No, whoever wrote those words on Emily's arm, did so with a bold swift movement that was definitely not self-inflicted."

"We need to talk to that headmaster," Swift said, as he shouted goodbye to Evans and marched out of the room. "O'Malley, with me."

Annie waved to the pathologist and ran after Swift.

THEY TOOK SWIFT'S CAR. AS ANNIE SAT IN THE passenger seat of the large 4x4, classical FM blaring out of the speakers as they sped down the dual carriageway to the very southern tip of the county, she couldn't help but glance around at the back seat and the very feminine coat she'd spotted strewn there as she had climbed in. Maybe Swift's wife had made a miraculous return. Annie made a mental note to ask Tink about it when they were back in the office. DS Belle Lock, or Tink as she was affectionately known, made up one quarter of their team. DC Tom Page the other. They had both welcomed Annie to their team with open arms in the middle of the last case. Tink knew all the gossip, as did Rose, the station receptionist and long-term friend of Annie's. She'd hit them up for it later. Right now, there was a dead teenager to deal with so Annie turned back to the front of the car and started thinking about what they had so far.

"So," Swift said, overtaking a lorry. "What are your first thoughts?"

Annie took a moment, letting the warm air from the car's heater run over her frozen toes. It was almost Halloween and the days had started drawing in before they'd even started, the grey mist very rarely lifted from the ground anymore. Swift pulled the car back into the slow lane and drove on at exactly sixty-nine miles an hour.

"So many things," Annie said eventually.

Swift laughed. "Can you narrow it down a bit for me, O'Malley? Let me get my money's worth!"

"Cheeky sod," Annie said, walloping him on the upper arm, her hand bouncing back with the tightness of his muscles. "You don't pay my wages."

"Nope," he replied, clicking the cruise control button and relaxing back into the leather seat. "But I brought you into our little team, I don't want to lose you now."

Annie smiled. "You're just worried they'll pair you

up with an actual police officer, so *you* have to start toeing the line!"

When Annie had been dragged into the case of the missing girls over the summer, it had been obvious then that Swift worked in his own unique way. A way that she'd never have guessed now, from the fact he was driving slower than her granny.

"Possibly!" He grinned.

"Okay," she conceded. "I think it's weird that our Chief wants this handled as quietly as possible and was ready to write off that proverb as Emily's suicide note. I mean, come on!"

"Agreed," Swift said, checking the sat nav.

"Do you think the school knew?" Annie continued, unzipping her boots and putting her feet up near the heaters, avoiding Swift's look of contempt at her Snoopy socks. "Not who did it, or anything like that. I'm sure they would have come straight to the police if they knew that. But maybe they knew it was a homicide and didn't want to push the fact for fear of parents finding out."

"God forbid their income drops because of a dead teen!"

"Yes, exactly."

They drove on in silence for a while, the thumping of the wheels over the tarmac rhythmic and steady. Swift took them off the dual carriageway and onto roads that became narrower and windier as they went. The 4x4 was built for this kind of terrain and took the corners far better than Annie's small Golf would have. And the heated seats were a bonus too. Annie still hadn't gotten around to finding out how Swift drove a 4x4 and lived in a mansion on a police wage.

"I also wonder," Annie went on, drawing herself back to Swift's question and picturing the red ragged line around Emily's neck. "How much her friends know about what's happened. And how it's affecting them. Who could possibly have that big a grudge for a posh teenage girl? A grudge that makes them drug her and string her up by the neck? Maybe her friends are worried that the same is going to happen to them? Do you think they'll talk?"

"I guess that's what we're about to find out," Swift said, as he flicked the indicator on the wheel and turned into a sweeping, gravel driveway flanked with conifer trees and the neatest box hedge Annie had ever seen.

THREE

FOXTON'S SCHOOL FOR GIRLS WAS JUST AS ANNIE had imagined it to be. It was right there at the pinnacle of the sweeping driveway in all its Georgian glory. A grey stone staircase, a symmetrical main building of matching grey stone, wings on either side that looked like later additions, and a bloody fountain. Annie thought back to her comprehensive school with its pebbledash exterior and broken bike sheds with a weird mix of nostalgia and envy. Swift whistled through his teeth.

"How the other half live, hey?" he said, pulling into a space in the small carpark to the side of the gravel driveway.

Swift's house was like a miniature version of this, only more Victorian gothic. Annie had thought he belonged to the other half he was whistling about.

Annie opened her door and stepped down onto the gravel. She reached her arms up to the dark grey clouds and stretched out her legs from the car journey, taking in the rest of the surroundings. Behind the school was a large grass playing field and beyond that woodland. A small bandstand perched at the edge of the trees, two younger students sat inside it, watching her with their perfect French plaits and fixed gazes. Annie pulled her coat around her body and followed Swift to the front of the building and up the stone stairs.

"It feels very quiet," Swift said, as he pushed open the wooden door and they stepped inside.

"Half term," Annie replied, her voice quiet in the large space.

The entrance hall could fit Annie's whole life in it three times over. The stone steps outside were mirrored in here, leading in both directions from a marbled floor, to a balcony around the room. Either sides of the steps were dark corridors, small signs depicted the way to classrooms and dorms. Annie shivered.

"May I help you?" A tall, thin woman, probably in her forties, with a greying blond chignon approached them.

"DI Swift and Annie O'Malley," Swift said, flashing his police badge. "We're here to see Mr Haversham."

The woman looked the two visitors up and down, her face impassive, though Annie felt immediately a sense of unease behind her watery blue eyes.

"*Professor* Haversham," she said, turning on her stiletto heels and leading them down behind the left-hand side of the staircase. "Follow me."

Swift raised an eyebrow at Annie, and they followed the woman's lead through a dark panelled corridor. Past a room marked *Staff Room,* and a couple of classrooms, and onto a thick oak door with a brass plaque that read *Headmaster*.

"Wait here," the woman pointed to the wooden chairs lining the corridor by the headmaster's office and then disappeared inside.

Swift giggled like a schoolboy as they sat down on the hard seats. "This takes me right back. But I bet this is the first time you've sat outside the head's office, isn't it? I get that good girl vibe from you."

"Hmm," Annie said, noncommittally. "Almost a perfect record, except for the time I slammed Jimmy's hand in the door because he wouldn't stop pinging my bra strap."

Before Swift could answer, the door swung open and a dark shadow fell over the corridor. The headteacher took up most of the doorway, he was broad in all directions, and his puce cheeks reminded Annie of a better dressed version of DCI Strickland.

"Professor Haversham at your disposal," he said, amiably, holding out his sausage fingers to Swift. "You can call me William."

Swift and Annie stood to attention. Swift took the headmaster's hand and shook it.

"DI Swift and Annie O'Malley," he said. "Thanks for taking the time to see us."

"Not at all, dreadful business." William Haversham stood back from the door and ushered them into his office.

The woman who had met them at the reception was so still, she blended into the corner of the room.

"Coffee, please," Haversham said to her in a slick

voice, then patted her backside as she left the room. Annie watched her flinch, but the smile never slipped from the poor woman's face.

In the office, the desk took up most of the space, bookshelves laden with works covered the walls. There were two small chairs set up on the opposite side of the desk from where the headmaster had taken residence, and Annie and Swift took their cue to sit.

"Don't arrest me for lewd behaviour," Haversham joked as he stretched out into his own chair, his body spilling over the sides. "Hetty's the wife. Makes a great PA with all the extras."

The man burst out laughing, spittle flying everywhere. Annie perched on the edge of her chair, her legs bouncing on the balls of her feet. Haversham peered at Annie with dark eyes through unruly eyebrows, he ran a hand through his thick, greasy hair, pushing it back off his forehead. Annie didn't smile back at him. She didn't look away. But she did feel a crawling sensation creep up her spine and nestle in her hair.

"Professor Haversham, William," Swift said, looking non too amused either. "What can you tell us about Emily Langton?"

Haversham's jowls were shaking. He steepled his fingers together, tapping at his lips with his forefingers.

"Her loss has carved a very deep hole in our small community," he said, lowering his eyes.

"Yes, I'm sure it has," Swift said. "How was she as a student?"

"Emily was a grade A student," Haversham continued, his eyes finding Annie again and running over her body. "Joined us here when I took over as Head, about thirteen years ago. She was part of my first cohort of boarders, I know her parents. It was a small cohort then, only ten or so students. But Emily was always top of the class, even of the day pupils too. Never gave any of the teachers any trouble, just went about her business like a good girl."

Annie didn't like the way he referred to this young woman as a *good girl*. She got up out of her seat to get away from his gaze and started looking at the photographs littering the only wall not covered in books. Unread books Annie guessed, the more time she spent in Haversham's presence.

The photographs were school photos, the kind where the girls were lined up in height and year order and told to smile, the building imposing behind them. Each picture looked almost exactly like its predecessor, neat uniforms, even neater hair. The year groups weren't huge like Annie's had been. Her own school photograph had been of forms rather than the whole school, because there wasn't a wall big enough in the parents' homes that could take a picture of the entire student body.

Foxton's current year was nailed at the top. Twenty or so girls lined the back row, Annie peered closer to find the face she'd spent the morning staring at on the trolley. There she was, Emily Langton, full of life and surrounded by what Annie hoped were her friends. She wasn't smiling, her eyes didn't meet the camera. Instead, she was staring off into the distance, a spot past the photographer that Annie couldn't see.

"Miss O'Malley?" Haversham's voice had an edge to it.

Annie turned slowly and saw both the headteacher and Swift staring over at her expectantly. What had she missed?

"William was just wondering in what capacity you're here?" Swift said, his eyes boring into her.

"Oh, yes," she said, smiling breezily. "Of course. Official police capacity as a psychotherapist. I'm here to talk to the girls who were friends with Emily and help them come to terms with her death."

And wheedle information out of you, she thought, though not out loud.

"Right," Haversham said, his forehead creased.

"It's hard enough dealing with the death of a close friend, especially at their age," Annie continued. "But when it's a homicide, that's a whole different kettle of fish."

Annie heard Swift exhale loudly as Haversham's face turned more sunburnt in Hawaii than salmon fresh.

Shit.

"Homicide?" Haversham spluttered. "What? What's going on? Bob promised me this would be over before I knew it, he promised me it would stay quiet!"

Good to know Emily's best interests are really at the heart of your concerns, Professor Haversham.

"Bob?" Annie asked, ignoring Swift as he flailed beside her.

"DCI Strickland," Haversham shouted. "YOUR BOSS!"

He stood up so abruptly from his seat that Annie

28

thought he may topple over backwards, or forwards come to think of it as his centre of gravity tried to right itself.

"Annie!" Swift hissed.

"What?" she mouthed back trying to look innocent.

She hadn't meant to give the big reveal away, but winding Haversham up was definitely a bonus.

"William," Swift said, gesturing at the swivel chair behind the headmaster that was spinning around in glee. "Please take a seat. I was just getting to that part."

Haversham huffed and puffed, his face calming a little back to a shade of red that didn't look like it might require a bit of mouth to mouth anytime soon. Annie tried not to feel too good about how riled he was, there was a dead teenager to discuss, after all.

As he grabbed hold of the back of his chair, and lowered himself back down, he gave Annie a steely look.

"William," Swift said quickly, hands laid flat on the desk in front of him. "Sorry that the news was broken to you in the way that it was, but yes, we have reason to believe that Emily Langton's death was not an accident or a suicide."

"That's utterly ridiculous," Haversham said, immediately. "The girl killed herself. Strung herself up to that tree."

Annie watched Swift's face and marvelled at how calm he was staying. "Do you know if Emily was seeing anyone, William? Any boyfriends on the scene?" he asked.

The colour rose once again in Haversham's jowls. "We don't have boys on the premises. And our students are not permitted to have relationships while they're with us. It messes with their grades."

"Is that something you can police?" Annie asked, indignant. "I mean, your young women are allowed out of the school grounds are they not?"

Haversham opened his mouth and then shut it again. He scratched at his chin with a dinner plate sized hand, pursing his sweaty lips.

"Of course they are," he said, eventually, smiling acidly at Annie. "But *my* girls don't want to be putting it about while they're in my capable hands. They're not slutty. They know what's good for them."

It was quite obvious to Annie what Haversham was implying with the words he didn't quite verbalise. She glanced down at her shirt buttons, the top two undone, and cursed herself for the unconscious action when Haversham gave a nod of satisfaction.

"We have reason to believe that Emily was engaged in consensual sexual activity on the day of her death," Swift said. "How can you explain that?"

Haversham rose from his chair, steady this time, his arms crossed over his chest.

"I think you've had enough of my time, officers," he said, coldly. "If you don't mind, I have a meeting to attend with the governors."

Swift stood and joined Annie as Haversham walked past them with a waft of Old Spice and sweat. As Haversham pulled open the heavy door of his office, Annie caught sight of his wife turning a corner at the end of the corridor and wondered how long she had been listening in at their conversation.

"We'd like to talk to the other Sixth Form boarders," Swift said, undeterred. "Can you tell me where I'll find them, please?"

"First floor." Haversham was ushering them out of his office with arms so hot Annie could feel the heat radiating through his shirt sleeve. "You can talk to Mrs Haversham, she'll give you the names and room numbers. Start with Una or Lily."

As they started walking back the way they had been brought, Haversham shouted after them.

"And you'll be done with this within the week," he said, no question. "Or I'll be talking to Bob about the pair of you."

FOUR

Mrs Haversham was slightly more accommodating than her husband. They tracked her down not too far from the headmaster's office, and she'd reeled off a list of names and room numbers before staggering away on her too high heels.

"Let's make a start," Swift said, scanning the list he'd hurriedly written. "Though this list is surprisingly short."

Annie looked over Swift's arm at the names in black and white. Emily had been in upper sixth, about to take her A Levels and head out into the world. There were nine names, including Emily's, only nine sixth form boarders in total. The other years were more fleshed out, but hadn't Professor Haversham said that Emily had been in their first cohort of boarders?

"How do we know who her close friends are?" Annie asked, squinting at the names and wondering where to start.

"Clever police deduction," Swift said, folding the list and putting it in his pocket. "We ask them, come on."

He started off in the direction of the stairs with Annie hot on his heels. Their sensible police shoes clacked on the tiled marble of the entrance hall and the stone of the stairs. Discrete signs pointed them in the direction of the bedrooms, and they followed them all the way down prefabricated corridors that reminded Annie much more of her own student digs than the inside of a Georgian mansion.

"The headmaster's a bit much," she said, as Swift pushed open an internal fire door to an identical corridor to the one they had just left. "What do you think he's more worried about? A dead student or the reputation of the school?"

"I think you answered that question by the simple fact you had to ask it," Swift said, stopping at a door marked 5a.

"Hmmm" Annie agreed, raising an eyebrow. "Who's this?"

"This is an Una Williamson," Swift said, consulting the list again before putting it away and hammering on the door.

"Jeez, Joe," Annie said, taking a step back. "Could you knock any more like a police officer?"

Swift turned his head slowly to look witheringly at Annie and slowly back to the door. He was silent. So was the room behind the door.

"Don't think she's in?" Annie said. "Either that or she didn't quite hear you."

Swift laughed and they both turned as a door further down the corridor creaked open and a small head popped out.

"Hello?" The voice was as small as the student it belonged to.

Annie took the lead, not wanting Swift to use his usual tact and scare the young girl away. She couldn't have been older than twelve, definitely not a sixth former. Her saucer eyes stared unblinking at the two strangers.

"Hi," Annie said, offering her hand. "We're with the police, could you tell us where Una or Lily are?"

The girl's chin fell, and her shoulders hunched. "No, sorry. Out." She shut the door quickly behind her.

"Rookie mistake, O'Malley," Swift said, once again checking the list of names.

"Huh?" she asked, following as Swift walked back the way they came.

"Could you tell us where Una or Lily are?" Swift said, pushing open the fire doors and heading back to the stairs. "You need to be more direct 'do you know where Una is?' or your suspect can answer no even if they do know where Una is."

"Right," said Annie. "Or 'what can you tell us about where Una is', probably even better."

Swift just cocked his head and gave Annie a small smile, never one to admit defeat.

"You want to know where Una is?" A voice at the bottom of the stairs stopped Annie and Swift both in their tracks. "You're out of luck I'm afraid."

Annie leant over the railings and was greeted by a mass of red curls, pre-Raphaelite, not unlike her own, though obviously cut and looked after by a hairdresser that cost more than a tenner. The young woman was dressed in uniform, which was strange given that it was half term.

"What can you tell us about where Una is?" Swift said, heading down to the entrance hall towards the student.

Annie laughed quietly and followed down behind him.

"She's gone into town," the young woman said, fiddling with the cuffs of her blazer, her eyes fixed on the marble floor. "Her and Lily both."

"Thank you...?" Annie left the space for the student to tell them her name.

"Florence." She kept her eyes on the floor.

"Did you know Emily, Florence?" Swift asked.

Florence nodded quickly.

"Is there somewhere we can go and chat? Do you have a room here?"

Florence shook her head. "Not here, but we can go to the common room, it'll be empty as there are hardly any students left over the holidays."

They followed Florence as she led them down the right-hand side of the grand staircase. There were classrooms this side, dark wood doors hid away labs and English rooms, a block of toilets and a sign for the library. Florence followed the sign and Annie figured they must be right in the depths of the school by now. It smelt like old wood and chalk. Florence stopped at another carved wooden door marked *Snug*. She knocked and waited. Annie caught Swift's eye and he looked as confused as she felt.

"Is this not a common space?" he asked, as Florence pushed the door open.

"It is," Florence said, and Annie watched a blush creep up her neck. "But sometimes students fall asleep and stuff, you know. I don't want to scare them by bundling in with a bunch of strangers."

As it was, the snug was empty except for the luscious furniture that looked like it cost more than Annie's whole flat. The walls were lined with bookshelves and paintings, a thick red rug covered the stone floor, there were squashy sofas, wing-backed chairs, and a real fireplace that was roaring and inviting. It made the memory of her old common room of grey plastic chairs and old lunch litter feel less appealing by the second. But Annie knew she had to stop comparing these schools, she was doing herself and her comprehensive a disservice.

"Please sit," Florence said, as she curled herself up in one of the burnt orange wingback chairs. "I assume you're police?"

Annie nodded but Swift took out his badge and held it out for Florence to take. She glanced at it but kept her hands tucked underneath her on the chair. Annie could tell Florence was just a young woman trying to hold it all together. She took a seat on the sofa opposite Florence's chair glancing at the large painting behind it depicting Salome and the severed head of John the Baptiste.

Odd choice of artwork, she thought as she sank right down into the cushions. Swift sat next to her and the movement of the springs had Annie nearly landing in his lap.

"Did you know Emily well?" she asked, when they'd

all relaxed into their seats, the crackle of the fire loud between them.

Florence kept her eyes on her knees, a slight tilt of her chin gave Annie her answer, but she waited for the young woman to talk.

"We used to be best friends," she said, eventually, her eyes flickering with the reflection of the fire. "We started here at the same time, boarded together, kind of. We were both five, though Emily is almost a year older than I am. I'm an August baby, she's... she was... October."

"That must have been hard for you both, being away from your family from such a young age," Annie went on. "Did you and the other boarders support each other. How many of you were there?"

Florence tucked her other leg up underneath her and seemed to shrink into the chair. She looked tiny, thin, like a sparrow and her eyes were fixed on the macabre painting behind Annie. As Annie watched her, she felt a cool breeze tickle the back of her neck, as though someone had just blown air under her ponytail. She shivered and turned to look, but the room was empty except for the three of them, and the door still firmly shut. She rubbed her neck and turned her attention back to Florence.

"It was different for me," she said, quietly. "I was always a bit of an outsider, but Emily made sure I had someone to talk to, she was always checking in on me, that kind of thing. She was a good person. A good person to have as a friend."

A silence fell over the room, just the crackling of the fire and the cooing of the pigeons at the window filled the space. Florence's pale face was shadowed by the wing of the chair, the window directly behind her and the material faded in places where the sun had drained the colour.

"There were four of us," Florence said as the fire began to die a little. "To start with. Me, Emily, Lily, and Una."

"Una and Lily?" Swift asked, his loud voice making Annie jump.

Florence nodded. "Lily was best friends with Emily. Lily Parker. They really were close."

"And you and Una?" Annie asked.

"Yeah," Florence said, her eyes lost in the flames. "I suppose you could say she's my best friend, if that's what you're asking? But we are all best friends together, I suppose. Well... we were."

Annie could see Swift jotting down in his police notebook, his pencil scratching.

"Each year more boarders arrived," Florence continued. "And the school grew in numbers. It was fine, for a long time, but recently Emily went from being the best at everything, to just kind of mediocre, I guess. The headmaster doesn't like to see his girls slipping. He's very strict. He wasn't happy with Emily's grades dropping, especially when she'd been his golden student for so long."

"And how did Emily take that?" Annie asked.

"Well, you can see for yourself," Florence said, sharply. "She hung herself, didn't she? Couldn't stand being told off by Professor Haversham or having to deal with her parents' disapproval. They were simply horrible to her."

"You said that you were always an outsider," Swift asked. "Can you tell me why?"

Florence shifted in her seat, pulling her legs up and hugging them. Not a great question to ask a teenager, but it was too late now.

"My name is Florence *Haversham*," the girl said. "You're the police officer, you work it out."

The headteacher's daughter? Annie thought, looking at her more closely now.

Seemingly unfazed, Swift carried on with his questions.

"Did Emily have a boyfriend?" he asked, shifting himself on the sofa to get more upright and toppling Annie sideways as he did so.

Florence raised an immaculately shaped in eyebrow.

"We're not allowed boyfriends," she said. "Dad's rules. I'm assuming you've met Professor Haversham? Would you go against his wishes if you were a young student of his? He has ways of making us stick to the rules."

Annie's skin crawled. What did Florence mean?

"How did Emily feel about that rule?" Swift asked. "The rule about boyfriends?"

"She was the perfect student, despite her falling grades," Florence answered. "There'd be no way she'd spoil it all for a man, would there?"

She sounded unsure; her forehead creased as much as her youth let it.

"Can you tell us if Emily was seeing someone?" Swift asked, ignoring her question. "We can keep it anonymous if that's what you're worried about."

"Look, I'm really sorry," she said, looking at her watch with wide eyes, her voice frantic. "I've got to go. I've got remedial maths class and it can't wait, Professor Haversham doesn't like his students to miss classes, not for any reason. And especially not classes he's put on for the stupid kids who can't get away during holidays."

There was a gentle knock at the door and Florence swung her legs around and sat up straight, sorting out her hair, biting her lips, and pinching her cheeks. Her eyes were wide, expectant, worried. A man came in, probably a teacher from the look of his rolled-up shirt sleeves and neat hair. Scars lined his forearms and glistened in the light of the fire. Annie watched as Florence visibly relaxed.

"Oh, Miss Haversham," he said, coming into the room and offering Swift his outstretched hand. "I was just coming to get you for class. I'm sorry, I didn't realise you had visitors."

"DI Swift and Annie O'Malley," Swift said, shaking the man's hand. "It's okay, we're just leaving."

"Of course," the man said. "Can't have the girls missing class now, can we? I'm Levi Wells, maths teacher, pleased to meet you."

Not only was the building better than Annie's old school, but the teachers were also vastly more attractive.

So much for no more comparisons, Annie thought, as she shook his hand too.

"Come on then, Florence," Levi Wells said as he held the door to the common room open. "Time for class."

With a waft of cold air from the corridor, the two of

them disappeared out of the room and the door clicked shut behind them.

"No boyfriends, my arse," Swift said, shaking his head. "I don't need your Spidey senses to tell me young Florence there was lying about that, now do I?"

Annie was too busy watching the closed door, thinking about the way Levi Wells placed his hands on Florence's lower back as he led her away.

No, Swift! No, you don't.

FIVE

Later that evening, Annie pulled the door to her flat closed gently behind her and headed down the stairs to the pizzeria below. Swift had dropped her back home after their trip to Foxton's School for Girls as he'd had somewhere to be that wasn't the office. She'd dropped her bags off, tidied away the paperwork from her desk, and laid out her camp bed ready for when she traipsed back up the stairs after tea.

It felt less pathetic these days, sleeping in her office, now Annie knew she was saving for a new place with the extra money that being a police consultant brought in. And her probation clients were none the wiser, as they sat in her comfy chair offloading their problems and setting their goals, that only a few hours earlier Annie had been laid out on a camp bed watching re-runs of Schitt's Creek and eating leftover pizza for breakfast, just a few feet away. Step by step, she was getting there.

"Hi Pete," she cried over the counter of the pizzeria as she took her usual seat by the window.

"Annie!" Pete called, throwing a tea towel over his shoulder and coming out to greet her, a bottle of Malbec in one hand, a large glass in the other. "How's my favourite customer?"

"Got another police case," she said, grinning.

Pete poured the wine and sat opposite Annie at the small square table with chequered red tablecloth.

"Tell me all about it," he said, taking the first sip of Annie's wine and then handing it over to her. "And I'll see if I can help."

She laughed. Pete had inadvertently helped out on her last case with Swift and had been dropping hints at her ever since. She thought he had been hankering after a change of career and had told him he wasn't allowed to leave the pizza business otherwise she'd end up living above one of those trendy cafes that only sold avocado on toast and that wouldn't do anyone any good.

"Don't be daft," he'd said over a large slice of Hawaiian. "It's just good for business, that's all. Capture a kidnapper, cook a pizza. Snappy marketing that customers love."

Annie had laughed and sighed with relief in equal measure.

"I can't talk about it yet," she said, taking a large glug of wine, herself. "We're under strict orders from the Chief, and he's not to be messed with."

Pete rolled his eyes at her, dragging his grey hair off his forehead with his arm. "Well, you know where I am if you need me."

He got up and started to walk away.

"I need you now, Pete!" Annie called after him. "I

need some dinner! I'll have a large veggie supreme with extra garlic oil, please."

Pete gave a salute and sauntered into the kitchen. Annie sat back in her chair and stared out of the window at the frost forming on the cobbled street outside. An old man shuffled past, carefully navigating the slippery pavement as his small dog wheezed beside him. There was a stillness to the air in October that Annie enjoyed. As though the world was righting itself after the joys and upheavals of the summer. She'd spent most of it alone in her small office come flat, feasting on fresh strawberries and lashings of Pimm's. Her Mum had called last week, while Annie had been in the tiny shower with a bottle of expensive bubble bath that she couldn't really use for anything except inhaling while she tried to wash without bashing her elbows against the tiles. Annie hadn't called her back and had been feeling guilty about it ever since. The voice mail had mentioned Christmas, and Annie wasn't ready to deal with that yet. But it wasn't any easier for her mum than it was for Annie, with half their family missing, it never really felt festive.

Still, it was only October now, the month of change, the month that Annie loved because there were no real reminders of her Dad who had fled and taken her baby sister with him. No birthdays to skip over, wondering if they were both still alive or which hippy commune or religious cult they were now living in. Annie had been seventeen when she'd last seen them, and not a day had passed when she hadn't wished she could find her baby sister, Mim. Though she wouldn't be a baby now, she'd be a grown woman twenty years old, sixteen years Annie's junior.

The smell of garlic and melted cheese drew Annie back from the sparkling pavement to the table in front of her.

"One veggie supreme with added garlic," Pete said, placing the pizza with a flourish. "No date for you tonight, I'm guessing?"

He laughed all the way back to the kitchen. Annie ignored him, as she always did when he brought up her love life, or lack of it. Up until three months ago, the only men she met were her clients, passed to her from the prison service for psychotherapy. Not really date material.

A rap at the window made Annie jump. Swift's mop of dark hair was just visible under a woolly hat and a thick knitted scarf. She waved him inside.

"It's bloody freezing out there," he said, shaking his duffle coat out over the back of the spare chair.

Annie was slightly regretting the extra garlic now.

"Do you want a slice?" She edged her slab towards Swift who had been eyeing up the food since he walked through the door.

"Oh, go on then, thanks," he said, lifting a particularly loaded triangle and biting off the point. "God that's good."

Swift talked through his food, his free hand covering his mouth.

"I'm lucky to have this place so close," Annie conceded, lifting her own slice. "What are you doing in my neck of the woods? I thought you were busy this evening?"

Annie had once dropped Swift back at home and knew it was the other side of the city, where the houses had their own gates and drives and sometimes pools and staff.

"Took less time than I thought it would," Swift said, taking another bite and waving a hand towards the kitchen.

He turned his attention back to Annie. A tiny dribble of cheese hung from the stubble that had popped up since that morning. Annie pointed to her own chin to let Swift know.

"I just wanted to chat to you about your thoughts from today," he continued, wiping his chin with the back of his free hand. "Thoughts about the school, the head-master, Florence!"

"It's out of hours, Swift," Annie said, raising an eyebrow.

"Yeah," he said, his attention distracted by Pete popping up at the kitchen window. Swift pointed to Annie's pizza, sticking a thumb up. "That's why I thought you'd be here, rather than in your office come bedroom."

The withering look Annie gave Swift did nothing to deter him. A quick flick of a smile and he was talking again.

"Also, I didn't really fancy heading home," he said, which stopped Annie in her tracks.

"Why?" she asked, her pizza slice drooping as it hung uneaten near her mouth.

"Oh, you know," Swift said, poking at the tablecloth with a short fingernail. "So, tell me, what are your mind reading senses telling you this time?"

Annie knew he was being facetious, and she knew it was probably to change the subject from his lack of willingness to head home, but that didn't make being called a mind reader any less annoying.

"I'm still more concerned with why the Chief wants us to keep it on the quiet, and why he hadn't already broken the news to Haversham that we're looking at a homicide and not a suicide." Annie kept her voice low, practically whispering out the part about murder even though the pizza place was the kind of midweek quiet that she loved.

Swift scratched his chin again. He stared into the space behind Annie's head, she could practically hear the cogs turning.

"Maybe he didn't want the hassle of having to drop such shit news on his friend?" he said, with a shrug.

Annie studied his face for a moment, the tiny lines around his eyes looked more pronounced with the darkness of the stubble growing too. He looked tired, she thought, and it was only the beginning of this case.

"So," she continued, flushing as she became aware of how much she had been staring at her boss. "The school? It's holding so many secrets the walls were practically bowing. The headmaster has a serious health condition, and cares more about his reputation than the fate of one of his students. Florence?"

Annie paused for a beat, she wanted to get her words straight.

"Florence has a beef with her dad, but I couldn't tell from that short meeting whether it was more than the usual teenage, parental, beef angst."

Swift laughed. "Sounds like an Emo band or an experimental dinner dish."

They fell into a silence as Pete brought out another veggie supreme and a bottle of red. He topped up Annie's glass and filled one for Swift.

"Enjoy your meal," he said, with a not-so-subtle wink in Annie's direction.

Annie felt her face flush again. *It's not a date.*

She kicked at the table with her toe, but Swift was too in love with his dinner to notice either Pete's winks or Annie's discomfort. Sipping her wine and eating the last slice, Annie sat in comfortable silence as Swift practically inhaled his own. As he wiped his mouth with his napkin, Annie finished her trail of thought.

"I also think there's something up with Mrs Haversham. More than the ingrained depression that comes with realising you've married a chauvinistic pig."

Swift nodded. "I got the feeling she didn't want to leave the room."

"She was listening at the door to her husband's office; I saw her hot foot it when he opened the door to let us out."

Swift raised an eyebrow. "Wonder why."

"Oh," Annie continued, she was on a roll. "And Florence was lying about them not having boyfriends."

"Yep," Swift agreed, eyeing up the menu and flicking it over to the pudding side. "Wary of us telling her dad, I suppose. Fancy sharing a tiramisu?"

"Go on then," Annie said. "Not just wary of us telling her dad. She's also sleeping with her teacher."

It was an inopportune moment for Swift to have taken a large swig of wine as most of it ended up on the tablecloth. He coughed and Annie waited.

"What?" he said when he'd eventually regained the ability to speak.

"Yep." Annie nodded.

"And this, young O'Malley," Swift said, his eyes still watering. "Is why I hired you."

Annie called Pete over and asked for a Tiramisu with two spoons. Pete's eyes twinkled more than the candle he lit in between Annie and Swift.

"Once again, Swift, you didn't hire me," she said, staring the DI down. "And why are we ordering pudding? What *is* keeping you away from home?"

A small line of sweat formed on Swift's upper lip.

"A work chat over the best pizza ever won't cut it with you, will it?" he said, wiping his mouth with his napkin.

Annie shook her head. Swift stayed silent. Pete brought out their dessert and backed away quickly.

"Look, I just don't want to be at home," Swift said, picking up a spoon and digging in. "Can you turn off your Spidey senses just for a little bit, please?"

His shoulders sagged so much they almost hit the table but that didn't stop him picking up a spoon and digging into the pudding.

"Okay, go on then," Annie said, grabbing her own spoon before Swift ate all the cream on the top.

"Good, thank you. Keep them turned off, just for me," he said. "They're too attuned to... well, everything."

"Hazard of the job, I'm afraid." She shrugged, tapping Swift's spoon away with her own. "Leave some for me."

"We maybe should have got one each." Swift backed away, holding his spoon like a sword, placing it on the table in defeat. "Next time?"

"Next time?" Annie asked, cocking her head.

Swift stared at her, his eyes moving from her mouth to her hairline and checking out everything in between. Then, as suddenly as he appeared, he stood and grabbed his coat.

"Right," he said, heading over to the counter to pay. "This one's on me, and I'll see you bright and early for a debrief."

"Yes, sir!" Annie laughed as she watched Swift flap with his wallet.

"Yep, nine sharp," Swift said, tapping his card and looking intently at the machine in his hand. "Bye then."

That was weird, Annie thought, as he scampered out the door and into the dark evening.

SIX

DAY TWO

"WHAT CAN YOU TELL US ABOUT THE SCHOOL, Tink?" Swift barked as DS Annabelle Lock swung open the door to the small incident room they had claimed for their case.

"Good morning to you too, Guv," Tink threw back.

Swift's face dropped and Annie coughed to hide a laugh. She knew how much Swift hated to be called 'Guv'. But, she figured, if you're going to shout at your juniors as soon as they entered the room in the morning, then you take what you're given.

"Right, yeah," Swift said, grimacing. "Sorry! Morning Tink, how was your evening? Good? Yep? Great. Right. What do we know about the school?"

Tink threw her stuff down on one of the chairs around the large table in the middle of the room, giving Annie the eye as she went past.

"What's up with him?" she whispered, taking the seat

next to Annie and grabbing a box of pastries out of her bag and putting them down on the table.

Swift caught sight of the pastries and hung his head.

"Sorry," he said. "I didn't get a lot of sleep last night and now I'm taking it out on everyone around me. Those look like almond croissants."

"Not for you," Tink said, offering one to Annie whose stomach had just rumbled loud enough to announce to the room that she'd love a second breakfast.

"But I just said sorry!" Swift whined.

"Too little too late, I'm afraid," Tink offered one to DC Tom Page and then tucked the box away on the chair next to her.

"Fuck's sake," Swift hissed through his teeth and he headed up to the notice boards at the edge of the room.

"What *is* up with him?" Tink whispered again.

Annie shrugged, desperate to ask Tink about the coat she'd seen in Swift's car but drawing the line because she probably couldn't do it quietly enough when he was in the same room. But there was something grating on him, that was for sure. Annie bit down into the sweet, generously filled croissant and turned her attention to her boss. The noticeboard was sparse, a photo of Emily Langton pinned in the middle of the blue material, a picture of her arm, a picture of Foxton's, and that was about it.

"So, what we have so far," he said, staring right at the snack in Annie's hand. "One homicide, Emily Langton, eighteen years of age. Died of asphyxiation from complete hanging, but she was drugged beforehand. Evidence of sexual activity, but no evidence of sexual assault. Doesn't mean to say it didn't happen, though. But she was drugged *after* the sex. Even as I'm saying it now, none of it makes sense. Emily had no previous record of mental health issues, no other drugs in her system, no boyfriend according to her school mates—though the jury is still out on that one, and she was a straight A student. *And* she had this scrawled into her arm, not by her own hand."

Swift turned and bashed his finger against the photo of Emily's arm in close up. "*Whoever keeps his mouth and his tongue keeps himself out of trouble.* A warning? A note of some kind? We don't know yet. Emily had been a boarder since the age of five, we didn't get a chance to talk to her best friend yesterday, a Lily Parker, she was the one who found Emily. We did talk to a girl named Florence though, another one of her friends and a long-time boarder. She's scared of something and very tight lipped! We also talked to her father, the headteacher of Foxton's, a Professor Haversham. Annie do you want to take the floor for this one?"

Having just shoved the last of her croissant in her mouth, this was a rather inopportune moment to have to stand and talk, but she nodded and brushed the crumbs from her trousers as she took to the floor. Chewing quickly, Annie swallowed and turned to the room.

"Professor William Haversham," she said, and Swift handed her a printout of the official school photo to pin on the board. She did a double take.

"Yes," Swift said, a wry smile on his face. "I think a little photoshopping has gone on there."

Annie pinned the slim, handsome face to the board underneath the photo of the school and turned back.

"Professor Haversham does not look anything like this," she said, a nod in the direction of the picture. "He's overbearing and quite aggressive, red faced, and rather overweight. Not that any of that has any bearing over this investigation, except maybe the aggression. Just so you're aware. Okay, so Professor Haversham took over the school thirteen years ago and opened a number of the rooms up for boarders. There were a handful of boarders from the get-go, including Emily, and each year he's grown the cohorts. He's built up the reputation of the school and people apply from miles away, and to be fair to him, the place is amazing. But he was fazed about something, and more worried about the rep of the school than us looking into Emily's death."

Annie thought for a moment, not wanting to leave anything out.

"Oh," she said, screwing her mouth up. "And he's DCI Strickland's best mate!"

A murmur of discontent spread across the two who hadn't known this already.

"Yeah." Swift said, taking back the floor. "So this is all on the quiet, we have to make sure no press get involved and if they do, we have to sweet talk them to keeping it low profile or we're all in the shit."

"Right!" Tink huffed back into her chair. "And we're just going to put up with that, are we? What about working with the press? They can sometimes help a case."

"Don't make my morning any worse, DS Lock," Swift said, crossing his arms over his chest. "Do you want to come up and tell us what you've learnt about Foxton's?"

"Not really," Tink whispered to Annie, grinning, but she got up and headed to the noticeboard all the same.

Swift smashed his palms down on to the table, stopping everyone in their tracks. "Enough of the attitude, Tink!" he yelled. "I'm not good on such little sleep and you're not helping."

Page cleared his throat and stood from his seat, crumbs from his pastry falling to the floor.

"Maybe we need to start this meeting afresh?" he suggested. "How about we all leave the room and come back in anew? Shake it off, like. Get rid of all our stress outside the room,"

He would look like a schoolboy fresh out of sixth form if it wasn't for the muscles bulging out of his shirt. Which made Annie not only feel her full thirty-six years, but also very unfit!

"Maybe that's not such a bad idea," Swift said, and he started to usher Tink away from him and towards the door. "You too, O'Malley, Page."

Annie followed Page and Tink out into the corridor that had a permanent smell of stale coffee, station coffee too, which made it a million times worse. On Page's lead they shook their arms a little, and Tink stamped her feet.

"What are we doing out here, Page?" Tink said, wobbling on one leg as she gave the other a little shake.

"Put some oomph into it," Page said, shaking his arms so much Annie thought he might do himself an injury. "Properly shake it out. Get rid of that pent up aggression."

Tink started to vibrate her whole body. Annie could do nothing except watch, her mind boggling as her two colleagues looked like drugged up youths at a rave with no music.

"I wasn't angry until you opened your mouth, Swift" Tink said, her face pink to match her jumper. "Wait, where is Swift, why isn't he out here shaking out his bad mood. He's worse than all of us put together?"

She stopped shaking, looking at the door. Annie looked too, but the Formica wasn't giving up any secrets.

"Oh my god," Tink said, racing past Annie and pushing it open. "Get out of my bloody pastries, you sod."

Swift waved a hand as he happily munched on a croissant, lounging in a chair with his feet on the table in front of him.

"That was such a great idea, Page," he said, winking. "Give yourself a promotion."

Page guffawed with laughter as Tink ran towards Swift, and Annie thought she might be about to knock the sweet pastry out of his mouth. But she stopped just before she reached him and gave his shoulders a squeeze instead.

"If I didn't love you so much," Tink said, heading to the noticeboard and batting him gently around the ears. "You'd be dead right about now. No-one steals my breakfast."

Annie took a seat now it was safe to do so. When she had worked full time as a psychotherapist her team had consisted of one other therapist she hardly ever saw and her manager, a sour faced woman called Marion. Neither of whom had much of a zest for life and neither of whom had ever suggested meeting up for anything other than boring work meetings. Being part of the MCU was a whole new life for Annie, and she had loved it last time around, and was loving it again now.

"So, Foxton's," Tink began, her game face on. "As Annie and Swift said, it's been in Haversham's hands for the last thirteen years. Prior to this it was a day school, still private, but no boarders allowed. I wonder what they did with all the extra space?" Tink looked off into the cobwebby corners of the room. "Anyway. Haversham has done some prefab alterations to the inside and created a floor of fifty boarding spaces in total. Mostly term time boarders, they go home for the holidays. Only a handful stay, their parents are abroad, that kind of thing. Though no-one stays during the summer months as the school is completely shut. Apparently Haversham rents it out for parties and the like. The sixth form, where Emily was, has nine boarders now. And from talking to the school secretary, a Mrs Haversham—keeping it in the family there, there are a group of three other girls who were close to Emily. Florence, Lily, and Una. All of whom are boarders, and all of whom are still at the school."

"Like I said, we spoke to Florence yesterday," Swift said. He was sitting properly in his seat now, his pen scratching on his notepad as Tink spoke. "She pretty much said the same thing. And, like I said, she's the Haversham's daughter."

"God," Page interrupted. "It's all a bit incestuous, isn't it?"

"Yup," Swift continued, he got up and went to join Tink. "Thanks, Tink. Anything else?"

"Just that the fees are astronomical and Haversham has upped them every year and it hasn't put anyone off."

Tink took to her seat, reaching over for the box and grabbing another pastry before offering it to Annie. Annie thought about it for a few seconds and dived in, grabbing a chocolate twist.

"Okay," Swift said, clapping his hands. "O'Malley, we're going on a jaunt to London, well the suburbs anyway, to talk to Emily's parents."

Annie sighed inwardly. "Are they not here already? You know, identifying and collecting Emily?"

"They've got transport organised to take Emily once the investigation is over. They were too distraught to travel. So we're going to them."

"Right!" Annie said, mentally preparing herself for a long drive that she didn't really fancy. London roads scared her.

"Page," Swift went on. "I want you to get a list of names of those who were staying at Foxton's on the night Emily was killed. Talk to as many people as you need to, I don't trust a word that comes out of the Headmaster's mouth."

"On it," Page said, gathering his stuff together.

"And Tink?" Swift said, dropping his chin at the DS. "Apologies for being a bit short earlier. I've got... stuff going on, but that's no excuse, so I'm sorry. I want you to talk to her friends, trawl social media, find out where she went out in the evenings and get on their CCTV. I also want some info on this mysterious boyfriend if you can get it."

"Sir!" Tink said, giving Swift a salute.

"Okay team." Swift seemed buoyed now. "Let's get

this done. And let's get it done quietly. Any queries from the Chief, send him my way."

Annie finished her third breakfast and grabbed her stuff.

"I'll drive us both," Swift said to her as they were leaving the incident room. "My car has more leg room, and we can chat on the way!"

"Deal," Annie said, squeezing past him as he held open the door. "But I'll get the road trip snacks. I can't be doing with any more pastries."

"Spoilsport!" Swift whistled as they headed back to the office.

SEVEN

Two hours later Joe was turning off the motorway and heading towards a North London suburb that Annie had never heard of. The bags of apples and mixed nuts she'd picked up as healthy road snacks lay untouched on top of the MacDonald's wrappers they hadn't been able to resist. As they passed through the outer ring of London, the roads started to narrow. The houses turned from grey council blocks to white stucco, tall, intimidating facades with impenetrable iron fences.

"Nice neighbourhood, looks affordable," Annie joked, staring out of the window.

The satnav told Swift he had arrived at his destination right in front of an immaculate town house. Detached. The garden was full of blossoming winter flowers and Annie had no idea how they were still alive given the first fingers of frost had already arrived. Swift pulled the large car into a space a bit further down and they both jumped out. Annie groaned, stretching up to the sky and listening to her bones crunching after the long journey. As Swift came around behind her, he gave her a look.

"How old are you, again?" he said, ducking out of the way of Annie's swipe.

"Old enough to know better than to rise to your teasing." She raised an eyebrow at him and grabbed her bag from the back seat.

Wrapping her coat around her to stave off the cool wind, Annie followed Swift as he stepped up the glossy tiled stairs to the front door and knocked loudly on the slick black paint.

MRS LANGTON WORE HER GRIEF LIKE A BADGE. Dressed from top to toe in black, her thin blonde hair was swept up with a pin, showing off her swan like neck. She ushered them inside at the wave of Swift's badge, her eyes searching the road before slamming the door shut behind them. Annie and Swift followed her through a checkerboard hallway to a kitchen so grand Annie felt like she'd walked into the pages of Homes and Gardens. Mrs Langton sat down at the island of her huge kitchen, and grabbed an espresso so firmly in her hands, Annie thought she was at risk of crushing the tiny cup.

Her husband, hidden in the corner of the room so quiet Annie barely noticed him, was the polar opposite. He looked like he hadn't shaved since the death of his only daughter. His dark curly hair sat limply around his forehead, and his clothes were rumpled and stained.

"What's this about?" Mrs Langton asked, looking pointedly at her watch.

"DI Swift and Annie O'Malley," Swift said, raising his badge to show Mr Langton. "May we take a seat?"

Mrs Langton gave a brisk nod and Annie took a stool at the marble counter next to Swift. She eyed up the coffee machine built into the kitchen. It was probably worth more than her car and she would kill for a cup of espresso of her own, but she didn't bring it up. There was a time and a place.

Mr Langton dragged himself from the sofa, walked around and stood behind his wife, his hand gently placed on her shoulder.

"We're looking at the death of your daughter," Swift said, bluntly. "We have reason to believe that it may not have been suicide and an investigation has been opened."

"Oh, God." Mrs Langton put down her cup with a crash.

"We were wondering if we could ask you a few questions about Emily? And we need to look in Emily's room while we're here too?" Annie said softly.

A low keening drew Annie's eyes from Mrs Langton to her husband behind her as he slowly dropped to the floor. She jumped off her stool and rushed around the island to his aid, narrowly missing Mrs Langton as she slid from her seat and walked over to the coffee machine, flicking the switch and filling the air with a rich aroma.

"Coffee?" she asked equably.

Annie helped an emotional Mr Langton from the tiled floor and took him through to what could only be described as a showroom. It was a multitude of creams and whites with cushions that had been plumped to within an inch of their life. She helped Mr Langton onto a sofa and leant awkwardly against the fireplace for fear of sullying any of the other furniture with her clothes. Mrs Langton followed them though, a tray of coffee in her hands. Annie took one and poured enough cream in it that if she did happen to spill it, the stain wouldn't be too noticeable. Swift took his black.

"Can you think of anybody who would wish Emily harm?" Swift said, as Mrs Langton took to an occasional chair with half a bum-cheek.

She shook her head. "We've answered all these questions."

"In light of the recent findings we were hoping that you might rethink and re-answer for us." Annie said through gritted teeth, her patience running thin with this woman.

"There was no-one." Mr Langton surprised them all from the sofa where he was shuffling himself upright. "Emily was a lovely girl. She had a few good close friends who she'd been at school with since she started, and I'm sure there had probably been the odd school-girl tiff, but there was nobody who would wish our little girl any harm. The four of them, Emily and her friends, were so close that they seemed impenetrable when you looked in from the outside. Florence kept them all together."

His eyes were so sunken they looked like dots amongst the grey skin wrinkling around them.

"What made you choose Foxton's as a school? It's quite far away, isn't it?" Annie asked, thinking of the two-hour car journey they'd just taken.

"The Haversham's are old family friends," Mrs Langton said, and her husband shot her a glance. "We wanted to help William when he started up in Norfolk. Show others what a good school it was. The Havershams moved for Florence really, needed to get her away from the school she was in. Bullying, you know, that sort of thing. They upped sticks and moved, and William transferred from the school he had been at for a long time. Emily didn't mind the distance, it's not like she was home every weekend anyway."

"Was she happy there?" Annie asked, sipping the coffee and trying not to sigh at how wonderful it was.

"As happy as any teenage girl is about going to school. She'd come home at the holidays sometimes, but mostly she stayed in school with her friends. If she wasn't happy, surely she'd have come home more often? Don't you think? I know I would have."

"When was she last home?" Swift asked.

Mr Langton answered this one. "A couple of days before she... before she died."

His eyes filled with tears, his face colouring.

"And how did she seem?" Swift asked, gently.

Mr Langton looked at his wife before he answered. "She was ok, a bit stressed, I guess. She was quite quiet, spent a lot of time up in her room, which is unusual for her." He caught himself. "*Was.* I mean it *was* unusual for her. She would often just flit in and out as though she had much better places to be. But the last time she was home, she felt like she was home. If that makes sense?"

Mrs Langton cleared her throat. A quick glance from Annie was enough to see it wasn't through a sudden show of emotion, the cough was directed at her husband and it was pointed.

"Mrs Langton," Annie said, putting her empty cup down on the mantle-piece. "Did Emily talk to you about boyfriends?"

She knew the answer before she'd asked the question. Who in their right mind would talk to a mother so jagged and austere about something as exciting as new love, or even lust?

"Emily didn't have boyfriends," Mrs Langton said firmly. "And please remove your cup from the marble or use a coaster."

"Girlfriends then?" Annie asked, lifting her cup back into her hands and guessing just what kind of reaction the question would garner.

She wasn't wrong. Mrs Langton shifted onto the other bum-cheek, her face turning such a deep shade of purple it brought a nice colour accent to the white room.

"Do not assume to know my daughter, *Ms* O'Malley." Mrs Langton almost spat the words out. "She was a good student who did not get distracted by silly things such as love."

Mr Langton was staring at his bitten fingernails, his eyes like the glass of the empty, brash vase decorating the fireplace.

"What do you think caused her drop in grades over the last few months?" Swift asked. "Did Emily normally have a drop in grades over the summer period?"

"Not at all!" Mrs Langton's words were strangled. "We don't deal in frivolities here, Detective. Emily knew that we were paying an arm and a leg for her education and she made the most of it. She made us proud with her straight As. As for what happened over the last few

65

months, your guess is as good as mine. I paid her a visit when she returned after summer to talk some sense into her."

"And did you notice anything wrong then?" Annie said, a wash of cold air blasted into the room as Mrs Langton got out of her seat and pushed open a window. "Anything out of the ordinary?"

"Not at all," she replied, perching back on the unyielding armchair. "She was fine."

Annie nodded, trying to keep her face from showing exactly how much she disliked Mrs Langton. Swift was doing a better job than she was.

"Can we take a look in Emily's room?" he said, directing his question at Mr Langton. "There will be a forensic team along as soon as they've finished in her dorm room, but we'd like to get a feel of it before they get here."

"A forensic team?" The colour had dropped again from Mrs Langton's face. "Whatever for?"

"Mrs Langton," Swift said, putting his cup down on the table next to a coaster, and moving towards the door. "Your daughter has been murdered; we need to do what we can to find the person who did this. I assume we don't need to get a warrant to search her room?"

"It's upstairs, first door on the right," Mr Langton said sadly, talking over his wife whose mouth had opened to retort. "We haven't been in there since Emily was last home. So you'll have to take it as it comes, I'm afraid."

Annie left the room without a word and headed up the stairs, Swift hot on her heels. Neither of them spoke until the door to Emily's room was shut firmly behind them.

"Lovely couple," Swift said, handing Annie a pair of blue gloves.

"Could be the shock?" Annie said, not believing it herself as she pulled the gloves on and turned to look properly at Emily's bedroom.

It looked like it hadn't been touched by anybody in decades. The bed was made to army standards, the carpet was thick and cream and unsullied by literally anything. There were no shelves, no bookcases, her desk and chair weren't covered in spare clothes and magazines, just neatly stacked piles of textbooks. There were no photos of friends and family, no pictures on the wall; it could have been a spare room for guests and visiting family if it wasn't for the sign on the door that read "Emily's Room" in large floral letters.

"No wonder she didn't come home very often," Annie offered as she opened Emily's wardrobe doors to rows of neatly hanging dark clothes. "This place is devoid of anything that a teenage girl could need. And I'm not just talking about her bedroom. There's *nothing* here for her."

Swift sat down heavily on the bed.

"You know," he said, sadly. "If it wasn't for the fact we have forensic evidence that Emily was killed by persons unknown, I'd not be surprised if this was a suicide. What an unhappy existence this young girl must have had."

"Do you know if anything has been found in her dorm room?" Annie asked, opening a bedside cabinet with a solitary copy of Lord of the Flies on the inside. She took it out and started leafing through the pages.

Swift shook his head and took out his phone, scrolling to his emails. "Nothing yet, but if it's anything like this then I doubt they'll find much."

"Maybe she just took everything with her to school? That's why this place is so devoid of feeling."

A small piece of paper fluttered from the book in Annie's hand to the floor. Surprised, she bent to pick it up, sitting on the bed next to Swift. It was small, A5, torn from a jotter with its side all frayed. Written on it in a neat handwriting were three names: Florence Haversham, Lily Parker, Una Williamson, with a tick after each. Underneath the names, the start of what could have been a letter: *I have a secret. I know something that I shouldn't and I'm scared. I need to talk to you. I can't do it here. I can't do it over messages. I don't want anyone else to find out. I have to do it in person. Please meet me...* the letter ended abruptly.

"What was going on between these four girls?" Annie asked, turning the paper over to a blank back.

"Come on," he said, getting up suddenly from the bed. "There's nothing else for us here and I want to go and find out the answer to that very question."

EIGHT

They arrived back at Foxton's as the blue suits of their forensic team were heading out the front door. Despite the growing darkness and the drizzle of icy rain, half-a-dozen beady eyes watched them from the shadows around the steps, talking in hushed words that Annie couldn't make out. They must be feeling the pain of one of their classmate's death, but Annie could feel the excitement buzzing off them. When the realisation eventually hits, that's when they'll need the support of the pastoral team and their parents. Annie made a mental note to ask Professor Haversham about the extent of their pastoral team. There may only be a handful of girls left at Foxton's over the holidays, but that kind of shock required long-term counselling.

"Sir," one of the blue clad forensics said, walking over to Swift and Annie. "There was little of use in her dorm room. Nothing really. We've taken some samples: hairbrush, mattress, carpet swabs and will let you know asap if there's an unknown donor. But as for anything else, well you'll see when you get there. We left it pretty much as we found it."

Swift patted the man on the shoulder. "Thanks, Dan."

"So, she's either completely anally retentive, which is unlikely seeing as children normally do anything they can to be the opposite of their parents at that age and Mrs Langton is the definition of anal" Annie said as she and Swift entered the school and headed back towards the dorm room. "Or she's stashing stuff somewhere else? How private do you think these girls' rooms are?"

Swift pushed through an internal fire door and held it open for Annie. "Considering Haversham told us that under no circumstances were his students allowed relationships, I'm guessing not very private at all."

They were back in the dorm corridors where the prefab walls made Annie feel as though she was hostelling through Europe all over again. Hoping that wasn't an omen, given that her year backpacking happened the moment she left the police force before finishing her two-year probation, Annie checked the room numbers on the door and stopped at Emily's. Though she needn't have checked the large 5d written in ink, as the blue and white police tape gave it away.

"How long does this stay a crime scene for?" she asked Swift, lifting the tape and opening the door to let herself in.

"Until the body is released, and the forensics have been completed." Swift followed in behind her and shut the door.

The forensic team hadn't been wrong, Emily's room was as immaculate here as it had been at her home. Annie pulled on another pair of blue protective gloves and started looking through the neat stack of coursework on the desk. Swift worked the other side of the room, lifting the mattress and searching the bedside cabinet. It was the usual type of dorm room, much like Annie's had been at university, though much tidier. There was a single bed, a matching cheap wood wardrobe, desk, and bedside table.

"Good to see the school aren't scrimping on quality furniture," Annie joked as she lifted some heavy textbooks from the wobbly bottom drawer of the desk.

Swift scoffed from where he was sitting on the bed, rifling through some dog-eared paperbacks.

"This mattress is as hard as my..." He stopped talking abruptly.

Annie spun her head around to face him, still bending over the drawers.

"What have you found?" she asked, the blood pumping to her head with the angle she was at.

"What?" Swift said, raising an eyebrow.

Annie straightened up, textbook in hand. "You stopped talking, I assumed it was because you'd found something."

Swift looked sheepish. "Um, no, sorry. I just stopped talking because I was going to say *as hard as my abs*, it was my saying, back when I actually had them. Now, less so. So, I stopped talking because I wasn't sure what the mattress was as hard as."

He looked pained, and Annie burst out laughing.

"It was your saying?" she said, through her giggles. "*As hard as my abs*? Swift, you're hilarious."

"Back when I was married," he shrugged. "It was kind of a running joke, but it was true."

Annie nodded, not quite sure what to say. She wanted to ask him about the wife that went AWOL, but a dead girl's bedroom was not the time or place. Instead, Annie gave him a smile that she hoped didn't look too patronising and went back to her search.

"Guess my abs weren't quite enough, hey?" She heard Swift say quietly as he shut the bedside cabinet door.

The silence that ensued was thick enough to get lost in. Annie put the textbook back and went to sit with Swift on Emily's bed. He was right, the mattress was like a brick.

"Sir, is there anything you'd like to talk to me about?" she said.

Swift didn't look up from the shelf he was studying. "I've said it before and I'll say it again, don't psychoanalyse me, O'Malley, thanks very much."

Annie shook her head and was about to get up and look though the wardrobe when something caught her eye.

"What's that?" she said, leaning into Swift and pulling out a little notebook from the shelf he was looking at but not really paying any attention to.

She lifted it over his head and opened the hard covers. The inside was spiral bound, a normal jotter or notepad. What Annie thought must be Emily's writing was scribbled throughout the pages. She flicked through it, there were the usual teen angst mind dumps, the hearts and flowers dotted in the margin. At the back of the book a torn page with a single sentence written *at the bandstand Friday at midnight.*

"Bag it," Swift said, getting a large clear envelope out of his kit and holding it out to Annie.

"You think it's the same pad as the page we found in Emily's room at home? The rest of the letter she was writing?"

Swift nodded as Annie carefully dropped the notepad in the envelope and then sealed the top.

"Friday at midnight?" Annie asked, watching Swift fold the evidence carefully and place it in his bag. "Was it a Friday she died?"

"It was, Annie," he said, taking the desk chair now. "What have we got? A young woman killed by someone she knew. A boyfriend, maybe, or a parent who lost their temper? Or a headmaster who couldn't deal with dropping grades or rule breaking. Or a random killing?"

"It feels too personal to be random," Annie replied. "Unless we're dealing with a very particular type of serial killer who likes to drug then hang his victims to make it look like a suicide, I'd say we're looking closer to home. *More so*, I think, as they tried to disguise it as a suicide."

Annie got up, thinking better as she walked around the small space.

"So, Emily had a secret and someone wanted to keep her quiet?" Swift asked, looking up at Annie.

"That would make sense given what she had carved into her arm," Annie agreed. "What was it, again?"

"*Whoever keeps his mouth and his tongue keeps himself out of trouble,* I think," Swift said, quietly.

"So what was Emily hiding? What did she know?" Annie asked, now pacing back and forth over the threadbare carpet. "Did she meet her friends and tell them? Do her friends know her secret? Did they see what happened?"

She nodded towards Swift's bag where they'd placed the little notebook.

"That," Swift said, getting to his feet. "Is the million-dollar question. Find out that and we find out who killed her."

NINE

THE DARKNESS HAD CREPT UP ON THEM WHILE they'd been searching Emily's room. Annie pulled out her phone as they exited down the steps to the carpark of the school. She pulled her coat around her and plunged her free hand in the downy pocket to stop her fingers falling off.

"Home?" Swift asked, taking the keys from his pocket and unlocking the 4x4 with a beep and a click.

He threw his bag in the boot, but Annie faltered by the edge of the gravel, looking out over the treeline that fenced the school playing fields.

"Fancy a walk first?" she asked, turning her head back to Swift.

"It's nearly eleven on a Tuesday night in a bloody freezing, rainy October," he said, raising an eyebrow. "And do you know what? I think that sounds like a perfect idea."

They headed off around the side of the school, crunching over the gravel carpark and pathway. The building loomed over them, casting shadows from the full moon in an eerie blue glow. A run-down bandstand stood alone at the top of the playing fields and Annie used that as a marker for where she was heading. Truly, she had no idea why she suggested a walk, when her feet were like ice and her hair was now a damp mop atop her head.

"Sorry about earlier," Swift said, waking alongside her. "About the whole abs thing. Not really appropriate for work talk."

"Shut up, Swift," Annie reprimanded him gently. "We've had less appropriate talks than that I'm sure."

Swift hummed in agreement and they kept on in a companionable silence, the grass underfoot squidgy in the rain.

"Do you want to talk about it," Annie asked as she reached the splintering stand. "About your wife."

"God no!" Swift spluttered. He caught himself and smiled at Annie. "Is this why you've brought me out here? False pretences?"

"No pretences, Swift," Annie exclaimed, wondering if actually that's exactly why they were out here when she could be on her way home in a warm, comfortable car. "Just wondering."

"Yeah, well leave your wondering for your clients, I've already told you I don't want therapizing."

"It's not a verb," Annie retorted.

They were both light with their touch, but Annie could feel the anxiety peeling off Swift in waves, so she decided not to bring it up again. Not until he was ready to start that conversation himself. There was a crackle between them that the wrong words could set alight. Like he said, she's not here to give him therapy.

Using the phone torch to guide her, Annie stepped up the creaking slats and onto the platform of the bandstand. Even in the gloom of the night she could tell the paint work was old and peeling, the boards in desperate need of a sanding and varnish. The playing field grass had been long enough to dampen not only the soles of her shoes, but the ankles of her woolly tights too.

"Why is the school in such disrepair when the fees are so astronomical?" she asked, completely changing the subject. "It's the dorm rooms all over again."

"I don't suppose the running of the place is cheap," Swift said, coming up the steps to join her. The planks under their feet bowed at the extra body and a clatter of glass made their heads turn in the direction of the shadowy back of the bandstand.

Annie directed her phone and Swift used his powerful police torch to illuminate the darkness. Two tumblers rolled around on their sides, an empty bottle of Grey Goose vodka was still standing, propped up against the vertical, green lichen boards.

"So much for *our girls don't let anything distract them*," Swift said, poking at the bottle with his foot. "Urgh, vodka."

His phone buzzed and he made his excuses, grimacing as he read the screen. As he swiped to answer, and started talking, Annie turned her attention to the woods behind the bandstand. It had started to encroach on the school grounds. The budding branches of the oaks were tapping the roof of the bandstand with a ghostly rhythm and the leafless brambles were snaking their way along the grass of the playing fields. A bird startled in the trees and took flight with a loud flutter of its wings, making the hairs on Annie's arms lift to attention. There was something about this school, about the grounds she was standing on. Or maybe it was just because it was past her bedtime and pitch black. Shaking her arms and legs of their pins and needles Annie turned to follow Swift as he walked along to the edge of the fields, his phone still pinned to his ear casting a bright glow to the side of his face. But something in the trees caught her eye. Another light. Not the white glow of a phone, but the warm subtle flickering glow of a fire.

"Swift," Annie shouted across the fields, waving to get his attention.

He finished his call and pocketed his phone, half jogging, half walking back over to where Annie was feeling daft for the prickles rising up her neck and tickling her hairline.

"Look," she whispered when he was beside her, pointing in the direction of the light.

Swift looked, pointing his torch to get a better view, until Annie pushed his hand down so the beam of light wasn't blocking out the one in the distance, or advertising their presence.

"There," she said, using her hand to tilt Swift's head. "Can you see it? The light."

Swift screwed up his face, pointing his chin towards the trees like Mr Magoo. Annie hoped he wasn't this short sighted when it came to his driving, otherwise she'd be getting the bus back later, if the busses come out this far.

"Yes," he said, when his eyes caught the flickering. "Where's it coming from?"

"Let's find out," Annie said, though Swift had already started through the trees towards the light.

The brambles were dense underfoot and Annie was glad of her boots but knew her tights would look like she'd joined a punk bank and was having a rebellious stage by the time they reached whatever it was flickering through the trees.

"Ow," Swift hissed up ahead, the scratching sound of thorns being pulled off clothes followed soon after.

Annie swivelled her phone around, pointing the torch at the floor, and saw a small dirt path over to their left.

"Swift," she said, tapping him on the shoulder and directing his gaze with her light.

They made their way to the path, it was little more than a track that had been made by footfall rather than diggers and hand, but it was better than the thorns and the mulch of the wet ground. They followed the track as it wove through the trees. Bare branches twisted overhead, mingling with the thick foliage of the evergreens that were dropping the water off their heavy leaves and onto the unsuspecting walkers underneath. Ice cold drips fell down Annie's neck as she trudged behind Swift, her excitement at being out on another case dwindling with each splash.

They passed blue police tape wrapped around the thick trunk of a tree. It rustled in the wind and Annie couldn't help but shiver at the thought of Emily hanging from the heavy branches. The tree was huge, a large craggy oak. Its pallid grey, brown trunk was dusted with algae and an arm was held aloft high over the path. It was the only branch that Annie could see that would have served as the structure for the noose. She looked over the pathway and the tree, a little thought niggling away in her mind, but she couldn't quite place what was wrong.

Swift held out a hand, stopping Annie in her tracks and drawing her attention back to the dark October night. She paused, listening to the rain and Swift's breathing.

"Look," he whispered, and she crept up beside him.

Past his outstretched finger, Annie could see a cottage, the uncurtained window the source of the light, a flickering fire inside looking welcoming.

"What is that?" he whispered again. "Bloody Goldilocks and her three bears?"

Annie felt her hackles rise again. The cottage was small, Swift was right, just like something out of a fairy tale. But it was the cottage of the wicked witch or the gingerbread house, not the warm friendly home of the bears, despite the warm glow of the fire flickering through the glass.

"What should we do?" Annie whispered back, her teeth starting to chatter together with the cold and the uncertainty of what was going on.

Swift straightened himself up. "We knock? I'm pretty sure we're still on school grounds, so it's within our jurisdiction. So, we knock."

"We knock." Annie agreed, her stomach tightening at

the idea of someone living there. A weird little house hidden away in the middle of the woods.

Why hadn't Haversham told us about this place?

Swift faltered but rounded up some courage and marched towards the door. Annie followed, less confident but not far behind him. The sound of Swift's knuckles on the cracked paint of the little door was swallowed up by the damp trees. They waited, listening for sound or movement within. A short while later the unmistakable noise of locks sliding back a precursor to the door being pulled open as far as the safety chain would let it. A ruffled looking head of dark blonde hair poked out, and Annie recognised it immediately as the teacher who had come to collect Florence from them in the common room yesterday. Levi Wells.

"Can I help you?" the young man asked, seemingly not recognising Annie or Swift in return.

Swift held up his card. "DI Swift and Annie O'Malley, we met yesterday," he said, real confidence in his voice now. "Can we come in for a moment to get out of the rain?"

The teacher's wide eyes searched the two visitors before he shut the door and undid the chain.

"Of course," he said, loudly now. "Please do come in, officers, and make yourself warm. And please excuse the state of the place, I wasn't expecting visitors quite so late."

The cottage was just as small inside, a tiled hallway led one way to a living room and one way to a kitchen. There was just enough room left for a staircase that looked like a death trap. Annie followed Swift through to the living room and the roaring open fire. The window looked like an oil slick from the inside, the night sky so dark and hidden by the mass of trees she could see nothing except a reflection of what was happening right in front of her. A small sofa, a low table, and a 16" tv furnished the room. There was little room for anything else. The teacher cleared up a pile of papers and magazines from the sofa and gestured for them to sit. Annie did, Swift stayed standing.

"Levi Wells?" Swift said, all his niceties vanished now they were inside. "We met yesterday; do you remember?"

"Sorry," the young man stammered. "Yes, of course. It's just been such a difficult few days. Sorry."

He held out a hand and Annie saw long deep scars that snaked up into his sleeves, twinkling in the firelight as she shook it.

"Can I get either of you a drink of something?" he continued. "Tea, coffee, herbal, water?"

They both shook their heads. And Levi nodded, looking around for somewhere to perch. With Annie on the sofa and Swift standing by the window, there was the doorway or the fire nook to pick from. Levi stayed in the doorway, leaning casually against the low-slung frame. His tightly crossed arms and darting eyes gave away how hard he was trying to stay looking nonchalant.

"Is this your home?" Swift asked, staring out into the blackened night.

"Um, yes, I suppose it is," Levi answered. "I've been here since the Haversham's took over Foxton's."

"You moved in at the same time?" Swift asked.

Levi nodded. "Yeah, they're kind of like my adoptive parents, only nothing is in writing."

That was a new one on Annie.

"What can you tell us about your relationship with the Havershams?"

"My mum was a waste of space apparently; I was taken into care when I was a toddler and passed between foster homes. I wasn't the easiest of children, so I don't think anyone wanted me for long."

Levi paused for a moment; his eyes trapped by the flames licking away at the blackened sides of the fireplace. Annie saw something pass over his face, an anger maybe, or more than that, a disgust.

"Anyway," Levi continued. "When I was a teen, Professor Haversham caught me hanging around the gates of his old school, I was seeing this girl and was waiting for the bell, waiting for her to finish. After shooing me away on numerous occasions, then realising I wasn't going anywhere, he offered me work, you know, groundwork, dogsbody, stuff like that. I practically bit his arm off, kept me out of trouble and I got paid for it."

"He *hired* you?" Swift sounded surprised.

"Yeah," Levi said, his shoulders squaring. "I was good at the handyman stuff. And then when he opened this place, I moved with them. Florence hadn't been getting on well at her old school and Haversham wanted to give her the best education, that's why he moved here. Then when I hit eighteen, about four years after we moved to Norfolk, they told me I could live here in this cottage instead of with them. Rent free, you know, if I helped out at the school and with the stuff they do during the holidays. Their parties, you know."

Levi's cheeks flamed and he looked down at his feet.

"And how long have you been a *teacher* at the school?" Swift asked, just as Annie was about to speak.

"Went to uni when I moved in here, Haversham home schooled me best he could, and put me through the exams. I think Mrs H enjoyed having another child around the place to look after, to be honest. Then I trained to be a teacher."

Annie heard a creak on the floorboards above her head and Levi cleared his throat loudly.

"Right," he said, clapping his scarred hands together. "If it's not too much to ask, I have a class tomorrow first thing and I should get off to bed."

Annie got up and shook Levi's hand again, noticing the trace of scars covering his skin. They shuffled in a line to the front door and Levi pulled it open, letting in a blast of cold rain. He shivered and ushered the police officers outside.

"I'm very lucky to have ended up where I am," he said, wrapping his arms around himself to stay warm. "God knows what I would be doing if Haversham hadn't opened his life to me."

Does he know just how much he's opened up to you though? Annie wondered as she caught the glimpse of a pale face and a shock of red hair at the upstairs window.

TEN

THE WINTER HAD COMPLETELY CLOSED IN ON ANNIE and Swift as they left the cottage and made their way back along the path to the playing fields. The air was bitter, biting around Annie and sneaking in through any gap it could find to seep into her already weary bones. She walked as fast as she could, but her legs were numb and her feet damp even through her boots. Swift stopped and waited for her to catch up as he hit the edge of the tree line.

"Alright, Rudolph?" he said, eyeing up Annie's cold face.

Annie ignored him and pushed on past, out into the open where the wind was picking up and blowing the rain sideways.

"Did you hear that we weren't alone in the cottage?" Annie shouted over the wind, across to Swift who had pulled up the collar of his coat tight around his neck and was walking with his head bracing him from the rain.

"I wasn't sure if that was a person," he shouted back. "Or just normal old building noise."

"I saw a face at the window," Annie shouted.

"Hold on," Swift replied, beeping the 4x4 open.

Annie climbed in and took the weight off her cold legs with a deep sigh. Swift climbed in next to her and pressed the ignition. Hot air blasted her from all directions with a welcome touch. They sat for a moment, long enough for the internal lights to pop out and cover them in a blanket of darkness, long enough for Annie's nose to defrost. Then Swift slid the car into reverse and swung around the gravel and off out the long driveway.

"Sorry," he said, as they made their way along the empty country lane, the bright headlights casting the road in a glow that dissipated into the trees either side, turning them into shadowy unknown. "Thought it might be easier to talk when we weren't battling the elements as well."

Annie found herself jolted by Swift's voice, out of the lull she'd fallen into with the smoothness of the ride and the blast from the furnace that was Swift's heater. With classical FM on gently in the background there was only so much she could do to keep her eyes open.

"Sorry Sleeping Beauty," he laughed "Didn't mean to wake you."

"I wasn't sleeping," Annie blushed furiously. "I was just resting my eyes."

Swift laughed even louder. "That's what my Dad used to say when he woke himself up with a loud snore during grandstand on a Sunday!"

It was the first time Swift had ever mentioned his

family, but Annie wasn't going to ask him any more about it.

"Back at the cottage," Annie said instead, shuffling up a bit where she had slid down into her leather seat. "I saw a face at the window as we were leaving. Young, female, I'd put money on it being Florence Haversham."

Swift let out a whistle. "So, you were right then?" he said, switching the headlights down as they approached the slip road to the dual carriageway back to the city. "Florence and Mr Levi Wells."

"Isn't that against the law?" Annie asked.

"It's illegal for a person in a position of trust to have any kind of sexual relationship with a person in their care, yes," Swift said, though Annie could tell there was a *but* coming. "But we'd need evidence before we went in all guns blazing."

"He put his hand on her back when we were in the common room, she was in his cottage!" Annie couldn't help but get het up. Where was Swift's sense of justice?

"Annie," he said, holding up a free hand. "I'm with you on this, I just think we need to concentrate on the case we've been given and if anything substantial comes to light over inappropriate relationships going on at Foxton's then we're all over it. But we can't drag Levi in on a whim."

Annie slumped back in her chair, frustration bubbling in her. A young, vulnerable child was quite obviously in a relationship with a teacher almost ten years older than her and there was nothing she could do about it.

"Do you think Levi has anything to do with Emily's

death?" Swift asked, as they cruised along the empty dual carriageway, orange streetlights flashing every now and then as they illuminated the slip roads and roundabouts.

"Possibly?" replied Annie. "If he's got a taste for young girls then maybe Florence isn't the only one he's been abusing?"

"Possibly. Though you need to be careful of your phrasing, you can't accuse a teacher, or anyone, of abuse when it's not confirmed. Not in this job."

"Can I say it if we're just having a conversation as friends?"

"Fair play." Swift chuckled a little and the mood in the car shifted.

"Bit of a weird upbringing too," Annie added, glad to move the conversation on. "I mean, some would argue that Haversham was asserting his own power over Levi by giving him a job and a place to live. It doesn't quite sit right with me."

"It doesn't" Swift agreed. "It's all a bit incestuous too. Florence and Levi basically grew up together. I wonder if the Havershams have any idea about the two of them... if there is anything going on?"

"If they do, then they're as much to blame as Levi." Annie shook her head, thinking of the vulnerable girl they'd talked to, on the cusp of being a grown-up but still so naive. "But Haversham was adamant that his girls don't have boyfriends, so I'm guessing they have no idea."

Annie tried to piece together the information that was jostling for space in her head. She knew the different strands of the case that they'd uncovered so far were still too thin and woven to be formed into any sort of semblance of truth. But the more they isolated each strand, the easier it would be to uncover the secrets that Foxton's held. And it held more than its fair share of them, that she knew for definite.

ELEVEN

UNA

UNA WATCHED INTENTLY THROUGH THE LITTLE PEEP *hole in her dorm room door. Since last week when their arse of a headmaster, Professor Haversham, had imposed a curfew she'd been bored rigid after eleven pm. Some of the other girls had flouted the curfew before they had buggared off home for the holidays, but Una was a scholarship student and couldn't risk being thrown out of the school. Her parents had been so proud of her escaping the small Irish village and the farm they called home. Una missed her parents with a void-like ache that had been unrelenting in the thirteen years she had boarded at the school.*

This evening she'd watched some year tens sneak out of their rooms, a fug of smoke and perfume following them down the corridor. It was so annoying, why did Una have to stay locked in her tiny, claustrophobic room? Everyone knew that Emily had topped herself because she was flunking her grades and her mum had come down on her like a tonne of bricks because of it. She'd been here quicker than a flash and Emily hadn't been able to show her face for a week. It wasn't the first time Mrs Langton had lost her temper. Poor Emily had hidden in her room for days, waiting for the bruises to come and go. But that wasn't Una's fault and yet now here she was being punished.

She slunk back to her bed and pulled her headphones down over her white-blonde hair and onto her ears. Taylor Swift blasted her breakup songs so loudly that Una would probably be deaf by the time she hit thirty. Her eyes shut; Una was dreaming of faraway shores and boys who were yet to break her heart. How was she supposed to be able to find a heartbreaker if she was never allowed out of her room?

Una thought that this was part of the reason for the curfew, too. Nothing really to do with the whispers of death, it was all a ploy to finally stop the girls having their own lives outside of school. Maybe that was what Emily had strung herself up over; not her mum after all, perhaps her dropping grades had been the result of a boy. She had blossomed early and was never short of an admirer or two when she went on a stolen night out. Provided she wore something skimpy, there was never any doubt in Una's mind that Emily would at least get a snog.

Una thought, perhaps unkindly, that maybe she'd get more of a look in now Emily wasn't in the picture. Built like a pre-pubescent boy, she was always left for the side-kick. Una knew this and was ok with it up to a point. But when Emily started flaunting two boys in her face not just one, that was too far.

It wasn't that Una didn't like Emily and wasn't missing her. After thirteen years boarding together, they were like sisters. All four of them. Florence held them together and Una had no idea how she'd cope without Florence with her now. If she could get away from her lush of a mother and arse of a father, that was. She'd tried to get hold of her earlier, but Florence wasn't answering her phone. Probably confiscated again.

"Goddammit" Una shouted, as she punched the floral duvet with the sides of her hands.

Throwing her headphones off and sitting up, Una decided to go get a drink. They couldn't stop her going to the kitchen, she wasn't a prisoner.

Una thought the first floor of the school, prefabbed to within an inch of its life was as though they were modernising it from the inside out like a cancer. The walls were made from the thinnest ply; enough to not be able to see through, not enough to make it overly private. She knew her neighbours' night-time routine better than she knew her own, teeth, hair, clothes, bed, vibrator. You couldn't keep anything a secret in Foxton's. Una knew that this was due to building regulations and that nothing permanent could be changed, but it felt oddly makeshift, even though it had been there all the time she had. It did mean that each of the boarding girls had their own space. Nothing like these American dorms that are on the TV so much. Una wasn't sure she'd have lasted thirteen years in a shared room, she'd have been the one stringing herself up by the neck, boys or no boys. She threw her dressing gown over the top of her shorts and vest and quietly pulled open her door.

They were allowed out of their rooms, of course, but Una still felt a little like a vigilante. The corridor was dark now and still smelt a little of the cigarettes and perfume left in the wake of the escaping boarders. Luckily, Una would know the way to the kitchen blindfolded, another perk of having been here so long. She crept out of her door, stopping the sharp fire hinge from slamming it behind her and letting it softly slide shut instead. The noise made the hairs on Una's neck creep as her eyes adjusted to the lack of light. She made her way towards the stairwell; the orange emergency light illuminating the doorframe like an eerie gateway to hell. The stillness of the air that surrounded her was stifling, Una felt her skin crawl and tried to shake off the heaviness. With every step, the lights from the door seemed to move a pace backwards. Una contemplated turning around and heading back to the sanctuary of her own room. But the very thought of turning around made her heart hammer in her chest with what might be behind her in the dark. She pulled in a lungful of air and tried to steady herself.

"Get it together," she said sternly to herself in a voice that echoed around the silent walls.

Even though she was the one who had broken it, Una felt her heart stop at the sudden crack in the silence. She moved her feet on towards the door, each step a little quicker than before. The silence replaced with the deafening pulse of blood as it pumped around Una's ears. Through this thumping in her head, Una heard something shuffle in the space behind her. She stopped dead in her tracks, her breath caught in her throat. A little whimper escaped through her lips as Emily's face flashed through her mind. Standing stock still, her skin prickling with uncertainty, she forced her eyes as wide as they would go *but she still couldn't see anything, the darkness was suffocating.*

Then there it was again. This time the noise was right on top of her.

Una didn't turn, she couldn't. The carpet fell away from her bare feet as she started to run towards the safety of the orange lit door. Running from whatever, whoever was standing behind her, breathing onto her bare skin. She hit the door with such force it swung open and crashed against the stairwell behind it. Una practically fell down the stairs and threw herself into the safety of the well-lit kitchen. She pushed the kitchen door shut behind her and leant her whole body against it. Her heart was pounding so hard she felt like it was going to burst, her chest rising and falling with the force of her breathing. Una stood there with her eyes squeezed shut until the world around her had stopped spinning.

A moment passed and the stillness returned. The blood rushing around the inside of Una's ears had subsided and she could now hear a similar noise coming from the other side of the stainless-steel industrial island smack bang in the middle of the room.

"Hello?" Una's voice sounded very small.

She was aware that the light was already switched on and there was probably someone making themselves a cup of tea. She was going to make a complete fool of herself looking like she'd seen a ghost. Cautiously she made her way round the island and into the back of the kitchen. It was empty. The noise was coming from the sink. A tap had been left on and was blasting water into the basin so hard that most of it was ending up on the floor. Una turned the tap off and grabbed a tea towel to mop up the wet floor. Down on her haunches she heard the kitchen door click open and shut again.

"Hello?" she said, standing slowly and wringing the sopping wet tea towel over the sink. "You left the tap on, flooded the place. Haversham's gonna have a fit."

Una turned to face the perpetrator but found herself in an empty kitchen, talking to thin air.

That's weird.

"Hello?" she said, this time a bit louder.

Una placed the towel on the work surface and walked around the island. She contemplated checking the cupboards but quickly talked herself out of it for fear of looking like a thief if anyone did walk in. Besides, people couldn't fit in cupboards, could they? There really wasn't anywhere else for someone to hide in the kitchen. It was big, but not that big. Una felt tears spring into her eyes as she forgot her thirst and ran back up to her bedroom, switching all the lights on as she went.

Safely locked in and lying back on her bed, Una felt the frustrations of the unfairness of it all.

Goddammit, Emily. I miss you. I'm scared without you near me. Una turned over on to her side and reached for her headphones.

If all else fails, turn to Taylor.

She caught a glimpse of something poking out from under her door. Tucked between her welcome mat and an old pair of trainers. Una crinkled her brow. How long had it been there? Had someone put it through her door when she'd been in the kitchen? Had there actually been someone else in the corridor with her? Her blood ran cold, why hadn't they replied to her greeting if so?

She turned the envelope over in her hands, it was warm to touch, cream, the kind of thick embossed paper that came with wedding stationary, or that your parents' keep in their drawer for the thank you letters you never wrote at Christmas. Her name was written in large loopy writing on the front. Una's face turned pale, her palms began to stick to the envelope, causing it to shed cream flecks onto her fingers.

"What the..."

Una recognised the writing immediately.

It was Emily's.

TWELVE

DAY THREE

Bleary-eyed and heavy legged, Annie walked up the station steps the next morning, coffee in hand, and pushed through the double doors into the reception. Rose, the receptionist and Annie's long-time friend, was talking sternly down a phone that she held between her ear and her shoulder, her perfect dark, glossy hair tumbling down her cheeks, her lipstick red and welcoming. Rose held up a finger indicating she wanted to speak to Annie, so Annie took a seat on the blue plastic waiting area chairs under a poster of a cat who had been missing since the first case Annie had taken on and waited for the conversation to be over.

"Now if you don't mind, I have work to do and people to organise," Rose said into the mouthpiece. "Good day."

She put the receiver down with a roll of her eyes and

beckoned Annie over, glancing around the empty reception.

"Sorry, love," she said. "My job seems to be fielding the weirdos these days, more so than normal."

"Maybe people are getting their grievances in before they hide in their winter cocoons?" Annie said, leaning over the desk and giving Rose a kiss on the cheek.

"Well they can bloody well go and hide in them now, as far as I'm concerned!" Rose looked tired. "It's bloody freezing outside and I'm not in the mood."

Annie gave her a knowing look and offered a sip of her coffee. Rose shook her head then leaned forward on her office chair.

"What do you know about Swift?" Rose whispered, conspiratorially.

"What do you mean?" Annie asked, confused.

"He was dropped off this morning by someone *in his own car!*"

Annie remembered the woman's coat, the lack of sleep her boss had moaned about, and the way Swift had gotten all defensive when he'd been asked about his wife.

"Do you think she's back?" Annie whispered, leaning in even further so no one could hear.

Rose shrugged, her immaculate eyebrows high on her forehead. "Gutted for you if she is, I thought the pair of you were getting on like the proverbial house on fire."

She winked and Annie's face flushed.

"I'm going to head through now," Annie said, before Rose could cause any more mischief, and she blew her friend a kiss and swiped her pass to open the inner doors.

The smell of stale coffee hit, and Annie followed the

general hubbub and chatter to the open plan office. Swift and Tink were leaning over his desk, studying something laid out over the top.

"Whatya got there?" Annie said, peering over from her side of the bank of desks.

The unmistakable lines and colours of the ordnance survey map gave it away. Held down, so it didn't roll away or fold in on itself, with a pen pot and a stapler, Swift or Tink had outlined what must be Foxton's boundaries with a thick red marker. The boundaries stretched all the way past the school where Swift and Annie had walked last night, a little dot marked Levi's cottage, and the boundary line ran just behind it, where the woods ended and hit the road. The playing fields circled the school building, and a few roughly drawn mobiles were scribbled on the opposite side of the stately home to the bandstand.

"Tink drew this up," Swift said, his finger on Levi's cottage. "The grounds are about three acres in total, so a lot smaller than it would have been originally. Mostly playing fields and a small piece of woodland."

"What're the mobiles for?" Annie asked, tapping her nail on Tink's ink sketch.

"Probably teaching space," Tink replied. "There's no record of planning, but then you don't always need it for temporary building."

Swift scoffed. "Temporary, my arse! Our school had mobiles that were older than some of the teachers!"

"You went to school!?" Tink laughed and got a side swipe to the shoulder from Swift.

Page picked this moment to enter the office, his hands full with a tray of Starbucks.

"Right," Swift said, standing up from where he'd been hunched over the map. "The whole team's here, what's say we head to the incident room and gather our thoughts?"

Annie grabbed her notes, and they went to the quiet hush of the incident room. The noticeboard had been added to in her absence. A picture of Mrs Haversham had been pinned next to her husband's above the school photo, and Emily's parents were there now too. She dropped her notes on the table in the middle of the room and grabbed a coffee from Page with a thanks.

Swift rummaged around his satchel and withdrew another photo, pinning it next to the Havershams. Annie saw the smiling face of Levi Wells. He grabbed his own coffee and a lull fell over the team as they prepped themselves for the day. Annie felt a swell of something in her chest as she watched the team over the lid of her drink. She'd almost not taken the role last time, a missing girl and a cult had felt too close to home, but she was eternally grateful that she did.

"So, what do we have so far?" Swift asked the team, his coffee finished and his serious face on. He stood at the front of the room, his shoulders obscuring Emily's photo. "Tink, what did you find out about where Emily would go drinking, dancing? Any CCTV of her leaving the school or anyone else entering on the night she died? Page, who was around?"

Tink gave Page a nod and he took to the floor, his

regulation shirt straining over his muscly chest as he leant to grab his notes.

"There are fourteen boarders still at the school, fifteen if you include Emily. Mostly lower years, but in the sixth form we have a Lily Parker, an Una Williamson, a Jaime Frost, a Clara Potts, and Florence Haversham, though Florence doesn't really count as a boarder as she lives in the west wing with her parents." He flipped a page over on his pad and carried on. "Jaime and Clara had been sent away on a two-day study field trip to the ruins out in Castle Acre as they're both studying history for their A levels. So that leaves Lily, Una, Emily, and Florence around on the night Emily died. Apparently, they're quite close as a group of friends, they're the longest boarders too. We spoke to them all again, to see what they could tell us about the night Emily died. See if they saw anything or anyone strange that they didn't recognise. Tink, you wanna go with this?"

Swift nodded. "Thanks, Tom. Tink, you're up."

Page and Tink swapped places. Tink licked her lips, no notepad in sight.

"They're all very tight lipped," she said, running her hands though her bright blonde pixie-cut. "But there's talk of a place in the city where they sometimes head out to, a bar that has a dance floor. It all sounded perfectly innocent to me, Guv, they need to let off steam and actually a bar is better than the alternative."

"Which is?" Swift asked.

"Buying a cheap bottle of voddy and taking it into the woods."

Annie thought of the empty bottle and glasses they'd

found in the bandstand. Often with no access to transport into the city, young teens were left with the option of making their own fun. Annie knew, through her work as a probation therapist, that this wasn't always the best option.

"There's CCTV at the front entrance to Foxton's," Tink continued. "There's no sight of anyone on it on the night that Emily died. But that's not to say they didn't sneak out, or in, through one of the other entrances that's not covered by camera. My guess is these girls know how to sneak quite well, given the state of their Headmaster."

"He's not the most approachable, is he?" Annie said, an eyebrow raised.

"He's not what they need," Tink shrugged. "In my opinion. And I just hope these girls have each other to talk to, and family who can help them through this, because he's got about as much compassion as my left foot, and his wife stunk of whisky."

The listening at her husband's office door, the clattering of high heels as they skittered over the hardwood floor, the slightly dishevelled look made sense to Annie now. She'd seen enough functioning alcoholics in her time.

Swift blew out a stream of air then turned to look at the board himself. Hauling himself out of his chair with a weariness Annie felt just by looking at him, he tag-teamed with Tink and turned to his team.

"Emily Langton, eighteen," he started. "Home life nothing to sing about, parents standoffish in their own way and Mrs Langton is pretty fierce when it comes to getting good grades. Emily had been at Foxton's since its inception with William Haversham, family friend of the Langton's, or Mrs to be exact." He tapped the picture of the stern woman with the nib of his pen. "So far forensics have thrown up nothing new, there's no foreign DNA, no fibres that are unusual, no trace of drug batches or where they were purchased. So, we need to find out more about Emily. We need to find out more about what was in it for the Langtons. Why really send their daughter so far away to a new school they knew nothing about, one which had no historic grades or reputation? Page, Tink this one's for both of you."

Page nodded, scribbling something down in his own jotter.

"Delve into the relationship that Mrs Langton said she had with the Havershams and find out if it was financial. The Langtons don't look like they're strapped for cash, but you never know. O'Malley, we're going to use your psychotherapy charm and speak to this friendship group properly, get some real answers out of all three of them. Can you drive this time, please? My car's... not here."

THIRTEEN

As Annie took the long driveway up to the school, she felt like she'd spent more time there than at her own flat over the past three days. At least this morning's visit was greeted with a bright sun and a crisp, cool frost on the ground. She pulled her Golf into the empty car park and killed the engine. Swift had pushed the passenger side chair back as far as it would go but he still looked like he was folded into it.

"What's the plan?" she had asked him as they'd sped along the dual carriage way.

"Speak to the three girls," Swift had said, turning down the Now Indie hits of the 90s without being asked to. "Una, Lily, and Florence. We need them to open up to us. To be honest with you, Annie, we're at a dead end unless we can get some idea of who Emily was as a person. Without any forensics this is turning into a nightmare. There are too many questions at the moment and not enough answers. We also need to speak to the Havershams again, something doesn't add up with those two and I have a feeling they're more involved than they're letting on."

Annie had turned the CD back up and they'd driven the rest of the way in companionable silence, Annie blurting out lyrics every time she forgot she wasn't alone until she had been too lost in Ocean Colour Scene to care.

"Are we getting out?" Swift asked, a pained look on his face.

"Yeah, sorry," Annie said. "I'm just getting my game face on, working with teen girls is *not* my most favourite thing in the world."

She opened her door and Swift followed suit, stretching up to the bright blue sky and groaning.

"Remind you of your formative years, does it, O'Malley?" he asked as they made their way up the stone steps and through the front door.

"Let's just say teen girls have never really liked me," she replied, ringing the little bell on the reception desk and leaning over into the empty booth. "Especially when I was one!"

There were no papers out, nothing on the computer screen. Foxton's obviously took its data protection seriously. But as Mrs Haversham came tottering out from behind the stairs, Annie wondered if it was less competence and more lack of actual paperwork in the first place.

"Can I help you?" Mrs Haversham said to Annie, her face a mask of Botox and a sheen of alcohol sweats.

Annie glanced at the grandfather clock in the entrance hall, it was only eleven and Mrs Haversham looked like she'd been breakfasting on the Asti Spumante.

"We're here to speak to a few of Emily's friends," Annie said to Mrs Haversham's pupil filled eyes. "Could you tell us where we'd find Una Williamson and Lily Parker, please? And we'd like to speak to your daughter again, if possible?"

"They'll need a responsible adult with them," Mrs Haversham retorted.

"Are you offering up your services?" Annie asked, her brain whirring trying to remember if a drunk adult was classed as having capacity for themselves let alone three minors. "Because I'm sure we can provide one."

"Hasn't Lily already turned eighteen?" Swift moved himself closer, making the most of his height and width.

Mrs Haversham was unfazed, she gave a shrug and muttered *whatever* under her breath. "They're in their rooms," she said, sniffing. "Go ask them yourselves. 5a and b."

She clattered down the hallway and disappeared behind the stairs. Annie and Swift gave each other a look and headed up the stairs to the dorms.

"I didn't really notice the lack of composure last time we spoke to her," Annie said, huffing a little as she reached the top step. "But Tink was spot on, she's an alcoholic, isn't she?"

Annie was whispering; the Headmaster's wife may be a beautiful, albeit frosty, lush, but she didn't want to advertise that fact to the students left behind for the holidays.

"I wonder if she's more with-it during term time?" Swift said, holding the fire door open for Annie.

"You'd hope so," Annie replied. "I'd not want my child being looked after by someone who can't look after themselves. Especially if I'm paying an arm and a leg for it."

They reached Una's door and knocked, hoping for better luck than last time. The peep hole darkened, and the door crept open. A mop of long, blonde hair greeted them, hiding a young looking, scared face.

"Hello?" the girl said, quietly. "Can I help you?"

Annie nudged Swift's intimidating form out of the way and introduced herself.

"I'm Annie O'Malley and this is DI Joe Swift, we were wondering if we could have a chat with you about Emily?"

The young girl looked Annie up and down, glancing across at Swift warily. There was the scent of sweet perfume and laundry floating out of the gap in the door and Annie could see how bright it looked inside, a vast contrast to the gloomy hallway she was in right now.

"Um, okay, I suppose so. Do you want to come in?"

Annie looked at Swift and he nodded. "Yes, please, Una is it?"

Una smiled as much as she could with her bottom lip between her teeth. "Yeah, that's me."

She pulled the door open and Annie went inside. Una's room was not only in stark contrast to the hallway, it was also the exact opposite of Emily's. Whereas Emily had nothing out on display and no form of individuality, Una's room was chocked with pictures and posters and brightly coloured rugs and bedding. A picture of the four friends as young children was tacked pride of place in the middle of the notice board.

"Not school regulations to keep it neutral then?" Swift muttered as Annie tried to find a good place to sit.

Notebooks and pens and a phone were strewn across the rainbow-coloured duvet, where Una must have been sitting working. The desk chair was a clothes horse, and the only other option was the floor. The thick pile rug in the shape of some sushi looked comfortable but Annie wasn't sure if she'd get up again.

"Sorry about the mess," Una said, her pale features flushing crimson as she lifted the clothes from the chair and scooped them into the small wardrobe. She sat down lightly on the bed, her legs tucked underneath her, her back against the wall, looking a lot younger than her seventeen years. "I wasn't expecting you."

"It's okay, Una," Annie said gently, taking the chair and leaving Swift to fend for himself as he leant against the door. "We're sorry to turn up unannounced like this, we just really wanted to talk to you about Emily. As I understand it, you were a good friend?"

Una's eyes darted towards her desk drawers, just a flicker, almost imperceptible, before they sprang back down to her chewed fingernails. There was no sign of Una giving up anything any time soon.

"Do you want an adult with you?" Swift asked, breaking the silence. "As you're underage."

Una shook her head fast and hard.

"What can you tell us about her, then?" Annie

probed. "How well did you know her? Were you her best friend?"

Una shook her head, her green eyes huge.

"We were good friends, very good friends, but Lily Parker was her *best* friend," she said, eventually. "She lives next door."

"And you all started here together, is that right?"

"When we were five." Una picked up her phone and started scrolling. Annie gave her a moment, thinking perhaps she was looking for an old picture of the four girls, but after a while it was obvious Una wasn't looking for anything in particular.

"I know this must be so hard for you, Una," Annie said, trying to catch the young girl's eye. "Can you tell us if Emily had a boyfriend, anyone she saw outside of school?"

Una's laugh was so loud and unexpected it threw Annie completely. A glint of something in Una's narrowed eyes gave Annie pause for thought.

"She liked the boys, if that's what you mean?" Una said, her voice had more body to it now, maybe these girls weren't as friendly as the school was making out. "She was always sneaking out to see them. I was gonna tell the other officer who came to see me, but I wasn't sure what difference it would make, we all know Emily hung herself because of her slipping grades."

"Una," Swift said. "Emily didn't kill herself. I'm sorry to break more bad news to you, but we know that Emily was drugged. We really need to know more about these men you're talking about."

Annie gave him a look that could freeze over his

normally extra hot coffee. The blood had drained from Una's face and she looked translucent, her legs up in front of her now, held up by her thin arms wrapped around her knees.

"What do you mean?" she whispered. "We thought Emily's mum had given her what for again and Emily couldn't cope with it anymore. You must have met her parents? The only time they ever came here was to give her a hard time. What do you mean someone killed her?"

Annie moved over to the bed and put an arm around Una's shoulders, feeling the bones poking through her t-shirt from her shoulder blades and the fragility of her youth. She felt like a baby bird, one squeeze would be enough to crumple her, so Annie lifted the weight of her arm ever so slightly.

"It is likely that Emily knew her attacker," Annie said, feeling Una's shoulders start to shake. "Or she was with someone she knew in the hours before the attack. Do you know where she had been on the night she died?"

Una's eyes widened. "She told me she was going out." There was the flicker towards the desk drawers again.

"Out with who?" Annie asked. "Did she have a boyfriend she saw regularly? Or boyfriends? Or girl-friends?"

"There was a couple that she was stringing along. She was unfair to them really, that's not fair, is it? Stringing two along at the same time. She could be a bit of a bitch like that."

Annie was shocked at the words coming out of Una's mouth, but normally when girls were mean about each other there was one underlying emotion. "Did you like one of them, Una?"

Una's face flushed bright red again as she nodded. "I would have given him what he wanted, but they always went for Emily because she had that kind of personality, you know, they thought they'd get what they were after."

"Do you have their names? Or any idea of where we can find them?"

Una looked back at her chewed nails, the skin around the edge of her fingers was red and cracked. The iPhone on the bedspread buzzed and Annie caught sight of the message that popped up on the screen, *Dan Barker* <3. Una's face couldn't decide between pale or flushed and had turned a sickly, sweaty shade of pinky-grey. She picked up her phone and swiped the screen. The silence in the room was punctuated by the keystrokes that Una hadn't turned off. Click click click. Annie found her patience wearing thin until Una turned the phone towards her and held it up for Annie to see. There was a contact, the same name from the message. Dan Barker and a phone number. Annie jotted it down on her pad. Una swiped again and held up another contact, a Stuart Hanover and a number which Annie took down too.

"These are the guys?" Annie asked, pocketing her pad and pencil.

Una nodded again, she looked like the energy had vacated her body. Her eyes were sunken, and her face looked drawn.

"Thank you for your time, Una," Swift said, making Annie jump. "We'll leave you to it now."

Annie scowled at him, they couldn't very well up and

leave her when she was in this state. But Swift had other ideas, he was already pulling the door open and heading out into the corridor. Annie paused, pulling out her purse and lifting a card.

"Please do call me whenever you feel the need to talk," she said, handing it to the young girl. "I'm just at the end of a phone."

She gave Una a gentle hug and shuffled off the bed and out into the corridor. All the time wondering what secrets the girl was hiding in her desk drawer.

FOURTEEN

"Sounds like Emily had a point to prove," Annie said sadly, as Swift slipped his phone out of his pocket and speed dialled the station. "As though she was trying to prove to herself that people wanted her, despite what her parents made her feel."

"Yep," Swift agreed, his attention turning to the tinny voice on the other end of the phone. "Tink, do me a favour and get a search done for a Dan Barker and a Stuart Hanover, both local, probably between 18 and 25. ASAP. One of these could be our perp."

Swift hung up and turned back to Annie. "Do you think that's what got her in trouble? Trying to make a point to herself, ends up dead?"

Annie shook her head. "I don't know, to be honest. Maybe it was a drug and sex thing turned bad. These boys are young, they might have been experimenting. Who knows?"

"I can tell by your face that you're not completely

buying what you're saying." Swift hammered on Lily's door and stood back.

"An idea is percolating," Annie replied, trying to make sense of what was going around her head. "Something feels wrong about putting the finger on these boys. Teenage experimentation does go wrong, but it's very rare, and it's even rarer that they'd then try to disguise it as suicide. Boys that age don't have the critical thinking that stops them just running away, not to generalise, but it'd be unlikely that one of them planned all that if they had a dead body on their hands."

"So you think it's unlikely to be Dan or Stuart? What about both of them together?" Swift hammered harder on Lily's door. "Lily Parker, are you in there?"

He turned back to Annie. "O'Malley, I've got the chief breathing down my neck on this case, I've already had too much time off work this past year and I have to prove myself, help me out here."

Annie put a hand on Swift's arm as he reached up to knock again. "Joe, I don't think Lily is in there. Let's go and find Florence instead."

He conceded, dropping his arm and following as Annie led them out of the corridor. The peep hole in Una's room lightening as they passed.

"What about how much you proved yourself this summer by bringing those abducted girls home?" Annie said, glad to be out of the narrow corridor and back in the expanse of the marble hall of Foxton's, the smell of wood polish filled the air as a small woman in a tabard rubbed away at the bannisters.

"It helped," Swift said, shrugging. "I had a *lot* of time off."

"And you feel like you need to somehow repent for having a mental health break?" Annie asked, heading down the stairs, careful not to touch the newly polished rail.

"The chief doesn't believe in mental health," Swift replied, scoffing. "He doesn't really believe in any type of health."

"Yep," Annie agreed. "You can tell that by his ever-impending coronary."

The old woman in a blue hairnet looked up from her work and an idea flashed in Annie's mind. "Excuse me," she said, smiling the smile she gave old people she passed in the streets to let them know she wasn't about to mug them. "Can you tell us the best way to get into the Haversham's private wing? We have an appointment with Florence."

She looked pointedly at Swift who cottoned on and drew out his police badge. The old woman stood up straight with a litany of pops and creaks and a big sigh, but the twinkle in her rheumy eyes was unmistakable.

"That little tyke been in trouble again," she cackled, coughing the cough of a forty a day habit. "You'll find her in her room. Sweet little thing, I've known her since she was this height." The old woman put a hand as far down as she could without having to bend again then started down the stairs and around the left-hand side towards the Headmaster's office. About halfway down the panelled corridor the old woman stopped, pushing at the wall. To Annie's surprise it fell back revealing a room behind it.

"Just through that door and up the internal stairs." The cleaner smiled. "Mr H is out for the day, so I think it's just Mrs in there with her, not that you'll get much sense out of her now it's past midday."

The old woman gave another death rattle laugh and went back to her polishing. Swift pushed at the door that had fallen back on itself and looked innocently like wall again and held it open for Annie.

"I've always wanted to go through a secret door," Annie said with glee as she slipped through it and into the Haversham's home.

The Haversham's private residence was as rich as the main school building, even more so as it looked loved. Dark floors and woodwork, burnt orange walls, colourful red Persian rugs scattered along the internal hallway that the doorway had led to. A shaggy, glassy eyed doe hung from the wall opposite a pair of headless antlers. It felt like a hunter's boudoir and Annie could smell the lingering smell of vanilla tobacco, though she wasn't sure if it was just in her head. A throwback to her childhood before her Dad took off.

Immediately to their left were the stairs, and further down the corridor were three closed doors.

"Shall we?" Swift said in a whisper, pointing up the stairs.

Annie shook her head and gave a nod to the closed doors. Swift shook his head firmly in reply and looked pointedly up the stairs.

"Are we going to have a nod off here," Annie asked, trying not to laugh. "Or can I just take a peek in the other rooms?"

"What if you come across Mrs H?" he asked.

Annie mimed the action of downing a drink and then pretended to be asleep. Swift bit his lip and tried not to snort too loudly.

"GCSE drama showing there, O'Malley," he said, as he conceded the point and treaded silently over the worn rugs.

The first door gave up a beautiful living space, replete with luxury soft furnishings and colourful artwork. A flush of envy rose in Annie's throat, so she pulled the door closed on the empty room and tried the door opposite. The kitchen was just as luxurious, but a sleeping Mrs Haversham, sprawled over the island in the middle, whisky tumbler almost toppled in one hand, a burned down cigarette in the other, took the edge off. Swift held up his finger to his lips and Annie backed out quietly with a sense of unease. What was it about the parents of Foxton's that made them so appalling? She was about to voice her concerns to Swift but he was too busy trying the third door, locked.

"Interesting," he whispered, trying to push his weigh against it. It didn't budge.

The hallway darkened as they followed it further down, opening up again to reveal a door to the side of the school grounds, out near the bandstand and the entrance to the woods.

"Let's go and find Florence," Annie said, turning and nearly passing out with fright at the sight of the young girl right behind her, her face so pale, her auburn hair looking like the painting Ophelia.

"No need," Florence said, looking wide eyed. "I'm right here. Are you snooping?"

"Not snooping, no," Swift said. "Looking for you. Your Mum said we could talk to you."

"Not here," Florence said, glancing at the kitchen door. "Let's go outside, Mum's busy in the kitchen and I'd hate to disturb her."

Annie felt the shame oozing out of the poor girl's pores and kept quiet about what they'd seen. Following Florence out the side door and onto the crisp playing field, Annie felt the cold biting at her fingers, the cool air opening her lungs with its icy fingers. She coughed.

"What do you want to know?" Florence asked, sitting on the steps of the bandstand, wrapping her arms around her thin jumper.

"What happened with the four of you?" Annie asked, jumping in before Swift could speak. "We saw a photo of you all in Una's room just now, and you looked like the best of friends. But some of the things we heard, I don't know, you all seem to have lost that spark."

Florence looked up through her eyebrows at Annie.

"Don't you understand how hard it is for me?" she said, her eyes filling with tears. "My dad is headmaster, the other girls fear me because of it. Emily, Una, Lily and me are all still friends... were all still friends, but I feel like I'm always on the outside. No-one tells me their secrets in case I go running to daddy dearest. Which I never would because he'd... you know, he'd not be happy.

They're like my sisters. I look out for them, and I care about them. I'm the best friend they could ask for because I try my hardest to make them happy. But I can't tell you what I don't know. And I don't know anything about Emily, because she didn't tell me anything. Your best bet is Lily, those two were the closest. I've been trying to find her myself. Lily was the one who found Emily and I want to make sure she's okay, but she's vanished."

Swift looked at Annie, concern apparent on his face.

"Not vanished in a bad way," Florence added, seeing the look. "She's okay, I'm sure. She's just cutting herself off from her friends when she needs us the most now."

"Have you heard of Dan Barker or Stuart Hanover?" Swift asked, stamping his feet to stay warm.

Florence nodded. "Una has a massive crush on Dan." She smiled, it was the first time Annie had seen any warmth in Florence's eyes and she couldn't imagine how hard it was for the young woman. "But Emily was stringing Dan and Stuart along because she couldn't decide between them. Sometimes, Emily could be a bit selfish like that. She didn't really see the pain she could cause in others. Una's my best friend though, and I could see what it was doing to her. Poor Una was mad with jealousy when Emily told us she'd been having sex with both of them."

Florence's face flushed and she looked wide eyed at the two officers.

"It's okay," Annie said, reassuringly. "We know you're all over sixteen, there's nothing illegal in sexual relations at your age."

"Try telling my Dad that," Florence retorted.

"I think your Dad is just looking out for you," Annie continued, knowing she was about to tread a fine line.

"He's probably just worried about you. You are his only daughter."

Florence's nostrils flared and she pushed herself up from the rickety wooden steps. "You don't know what you're talking about. You wouldn't understand how hard it is to live with my parents. They can't stand secrets and lies, they'd rather we were unable to talk at all, than anything untrue crosses our lips," she said, heading back to the side door. "You'll probably find Lily in the woods. I'm sure she'll be able to tell you more about Emily's boyfriends. If you do find her, please can you ask her to come and talk to me? I... miss her."

With her head down and her slight body shaking in the cold, Florence disappeared into her home with the clatter of the lock following soon after.

"To the woods?" Swift asked.

Annie nodded, her gaze still watching the door Florence had disappeared into. *What wouldn't I understand, Florence? What aren't you telling us?*

FIFTEEN

In the light of day, the woods were beautiful. Branches twisted around each other like lovers' fingers. Underfoot was soft with the coils of bracken and the mulch from the summer glut dampened by the impending autumn. They found the entrance to the path easier this time, too, and headed off into the trees to try and find the elusive Lily.

"Do you think Lily is coping okay?" Swift asked, holding back a branch so it didn't swing off him and smack Annie in the face. "Given what Florence just said?"

Annie took the branch and let it go gently once she'd passed.

"Finding your best friend hanging dead by her neck is not something an adult would be able to deal with, let alone a teenager whose own coping mechanisms haven't yet developed past anger, lashing out, and drinking yourself into a coma."

"Wait," Swift said, turning abruptly back to Annie.

"Our coping mechanisms are supposed to develop *past* these things?"

He smiled wryly and carried on walking towards the infamous tree and Levi's cottage hidden in the woods. It wasn't long until they turned the corner and spotted the tree up ahead. At its base sat another young girl, her black hair pulled back in a gymnast ponytail, her face buried in her knees. Annie and Swift looked at each other and sped towards her.

"Lily?" Swift said, whipping off his coat and putting it over the shoulders of the girl, covering her thin jumper. "Lily Parker? I'm DI Swift and this is Annie O'Malley. Can we take you somewhere warmer?"

Lily looked up from her knees with bloodshot eyes and lips that were tinted blue. She gave a slight nod and Swift helped her up from the woodland floor. She was tall and lithe, but her tight jeans and sweater gave away the blossoming adult in her. She looked older than her friends, more worldly. Lily looked up through her eyelashes at Swift, her lips pouting slightly, as she huddled into his body, his arm around her shoulder. Annie resisted the urge to roll her eyes, trying to feel compassion for the girl who'd discovered her best friend dead. But the speed with which she'd switched from grieving friend to absolute vixen when she'd spotted Swift had been whiplash inducing. Annie watched from behind as Swift carefully walked Lily out of the woods and around the front of the school, despite the girl's height her head rested perfectly under his arm. They took the stairs to the entrance hall and around through to the common room.

As Swift sat Lily down on the squashy sofa in front of the painting of Salome and beside the fire, he looked about, searching for something he obviously couldn't find as he turned to Annie.

"Can you go get some hot drinks?" he asked, lifting a blanket from the back of the wingback and placing it over Lily's legs.

Annie said nothing in reply, sitting on the wingback opposite and folding her arms across her chest.

"I'm fine," Lily croaked, in a voice that sounded anything but. "I don't really drink hot drinks anyway."

She gave Swift a sweet smile that dropped as soon as he turned to sit down, leaving Annie with a rush of terror she hadn't felt since her own days in sixth form. Taking a deep breath, Annie reminded herself that she was the adult in this situation, she wasn't a teenager anymore, trying to hide from the world because it was mean and unkind and way too interested in her kidnapped sister and missing father. Annie had endured the whispered looks and the hushed gazes back then, but she needed to up her game now and remember where she was. This wasn't about her; it was about Emily Langton and the best friend who had found her.

"Why were you out there just now?" Swift asked Lily whose face had changed from translucent to glowing in the time she'd been snuggled up by the fire. "It's cold out there, you could have gotten ill. It's not a walk in the park, you know, hypothermia."

Lily looked suitably chastised with the doe-eyed pout she gave Swift. Annie's own eyes would have rolled all the way back in her head if she'd not been in full on concentrating mode.

"I just miss her, you know?" Lily said, running her fingers through her thick ponytail. "I wanted to be close to her. To..."

A flicker of something ran over Lily's face and she looked eighteen and scared and Annie hated herself a little for being annoyed at the girl's flirting. It was a coping mechanism, nothing else. Something to take her mind off the fact her best friend was dead, flirting with the, undeniably attractive, older man in charge.

"Lily," Annie said, softly. "Can you tell us what happened the night Emily died? What do you think she was doing out in the woods after dark?"

Lily dragged her bottom lip into her mouth and started chewing frantically.

"Lily?" Annie said, again. She reached forwards instinctively as the young girl's eyes started to water. Lily flinched, moving away from Annie's outstretched arms and Annie filed that reaction away for later. "Are you okay?"

Lily shook her head, her bottom lip still hidden beneath her teeth. "It's my fault Emily is dead," she said, eventually, the tears streaming down her cheeks. "If I had only..."

The room fell into silence again, the only noise the crackle of the fire and the calling of the wood pigeons through the window. This time it was Swift who leant forward, placing his hands over Lily's and moving onto the sofa next to her. She didn't move, she didn't lean into

Swift. Lily's whole body was tense, like a coiled spring ready to jump away.

"Can you tell us what you mean?" Swift asked.

Lilly peeled her hands from underneath the detective's and stood up abruptly.

"No," she said, wiping her face with her hands. "But I can show you."

And she disappeared out of the room, slamming the heavy door shut behind her.

"Do you think she'll come back?" he asked Annie.

Annie nodded. "Did you see the way she flinched when I went to comfort her? And the way she sat when you took the spot next to her? It was a complete one-eighty from how she'd been with you earlier."

"Yeah, that was weird. What are you thinking?"

"I don't know if it was just because she wasn't holding the power anymore." Annie shook her head, deep in thought staring at the flickering flames. "Or if there is something more going on with these young women."

"Like what?"

Annie drew her eyes away from the magnetism of the fire. "I don't know, but I get weird vibes from this school. Like there's a secret it's hiding, and these girls have something to do with it."

"Abuse, you mean?"

"Maybe. I'm not sure." Annie was going to add that she felt it centred around the headmaster when Lily burst back into the room with a large envelope gripped tightly in her hand. She held it out to Swift and buried herself back on the sofa under the blanket, shivering from head to toe.

Annie remembered the blast of cool air that she had felt the previous day, sitting where Lily was now, as Lily rubbed the back of her neck and pulled the blanket up higher.

Swift glanced at the envelope, his head turning between Lily and whatever it was she had just handed him. He pulled out what was inside and read.

"Where did you get this?" he asked, the edge back in his voice so Annie knew it was important.

"Una has one too," Lily said, the words shaky.

Swift held it out to Annie so she could see what it was. It was the letter they had found in Emily's room, only this one was written on card and addressed to Lily.

Lily, I have a secret. I know something that I shouldn't and I'm scared. I need to talk to you. I cant do it here. I can't do it over messages. I don't want anyone else to find out. I have to do it in person. Please meet me on Friday at the bandstand at midnight.

Exx

"Is this Emily's handwriting, Lily?" Annie asked, looking from the letter to Swift.

"Yes." Lily nodded. "If only I had gone, if only I had been there at midnight, I could have stopped whoever it was who killed her."

Lily broke down again, covering her face in her hands and the blanket.

"You said Una got one of these too," Annie asked. "Did *she* go and meet Emily, do you know?"

The blanket swayed from side to side as Lily shook her head.

126

"We couldn't," she said in almost a whisper. "We didn't know. We didn't have the letters in time."

Annie stole a glance at Swift.

"What do you mean, Lily?" Swift asked. "You didn't have the letters in time for what?"

"To save her!" Lily shouted, taking Annie aback, tears and spit flew from her lips. "Someone slid this under my dorm room door yesterday, and they did the same to Una."

"Who did, Lily? Did you see?" Swift asked, but Lily shook her head quickly, her eyes darted to the common room door as it slid open.

"What's going on here?"

It was Levi Wells, cast in a shadow and taking up most of the doorframe. He stepped boldly into the room and sat down with Lily, placing his arm around her shoulders.

"Come on, Lily," he said, lifting the girl to her feet. "Let's get you to your room."

He walked her towards the corridor, stopping only momentarily to look back at Annie and Swift. "You should know better than to keep interviewing minors without a responsible adult present." And then they were gone.

Swift blew air out between his front teeth. "Let's bag this up and get it tested for fingerprints. Annie?"

Annie pulled on a single glove from her pocket and held the letter while Swift grabbed an evidence bag. The writing was looped and slanted, but not rushed. Emily had taken care when she wrote it and Annie wondered who else, along with Una and Lily had received one. She could hazard a guess at at least one other student.

"Can you go and put this in the car," Swift said, handing the sealed bag to Annie. "I'll meet you back there in five."

"Where are *you* going?" she asked, not taking the evidence from him.

Swift lifted his eyebrows as if to say *don't ask*. But Annie didn't take much notice and didn't make a move to leave.

"Oh, for god's sake," he said, shaking his head and putting the evidence in his own bag. "The cleaner said that Haversham is out for the day, I'm going to go check out his office."

"And leave me behind?" Annie hissed back. "I don't think so!"

SIXTEEN

When Swift said he was going to check out Haversham's office, Annie thought he meant his Headmaster's office. So she was pleasantly surprised to find herself sneaking through the internal door to the Haversham's private residence once again.

"Keep an eye out," Swift whispered, lifting a set of long, thin keys from his bag and sliding one silently into the locked door that held his private study.

Annie glanced around the dark corridor. Mrs Haversham was still comatose on the kitchen island, so it was just Florence she was looking out for. She could be with Levi, but the way he'd swooped in just then to rescue Lily made Annie wonder if he was spreading his love a little further than just Florence, especially with the speed he whisked Lily away when he saw who she was talking to. With a click and a clunk, the door to Haversham's office swung open and Swift grabbed Annie's arm and dragged her inside, shutting it silently behind them. He flicked a switch on and the room was illuminated.

Much like the rest of the private residence, Haversham's office was rich in colours and dark woods. The dark green walls were lined with bookshelves and a grandmother clock ticked noisily in the corner, a relative of the grandfather clock out in the entrance of the school, perhaps. Swift went straight over to the desk and booted up the Mac. Annie found herself, head tilted, reading the spines of the books lining the shelves. *Lazenby, de Musset, Marquis de Sade.* Pulling out one of the faded, material dust covers Annie flicked through depictions of early sado-masochism and quickly slid the book back where she'd found it.

"I'm sensing a theme," she said, taking a walk around the edge of the study.

The walls that weren't covered in bookshelves had paintings and prints of different ages and sizes but similar themes. Women bound and gagged, half naked, come to bed eyes staring at the viewer. It made Annie feel uncomfortable and set alarm bells ringing in her head.

"Theme very much continued over here," Swift replied, clicking the mouse erratically.

"What?" Annie asked, heading over to peer over Swift's shoulder. "He doesn't have a password lock?"

Swift flicked a post-it stuck to the bottom of the screen with the word FlorenceH123 written on it in blue ink.

"That's just asking for trouble," Swift said, going back to the history tab on Google Chrome.

The list was painfully inevitable, though a lot less discerning than his bookshelf reading material.

"Urgh," Annie said, pointing to one particularly stomach-churning search topic. "Really?"

"Each to their own, O'Malley," Swift said, wryly. "Each to their own."

"Is there anything concrete that we can pin on Haversham?"

Swift looked up from the screen. "Aside from the grim love for 'teenage' orgy porn, you mean?"

"Jeez." Annie screwed up her face. "But like you said, personal taste, but it doesn't mean he's a killer."

"No," Swift agreed, clicking the mouse from the internet tab and opening up the blue documents folder in the corner of the screen. "But look at this."

He clicked once and a folder opened up, entitled *Summer party 2021*. The folder had a couple of word docs and a spreadsheet, not overly high tech but Swift clicked the xls. named *attendees*.

A green spreadsheet opened, a list of initials down the left-hand side column, next to it a column with sporadic ticks entitled *paid*.

"I remember Haversham and Levi both talking about the Foxton summer parties," Annie said, watching as Swift opened up the word document. "Haversham obviously takes the organisation of them very seriously."

The first word document was an itinerary of the weekend long celebrations. It was set out like a festival line-up with House Party in bold letter emblazoned along the top. Friday's entertainment looked to be coming from a burlesque dancer named Tiffany Tease. Saturday listed things that Annie had no idea if they were band names or instructions; full-course, unicorn, bull, sprinkles... and on it went into Sunday when it would apparently culminate in a gigantic buffet. It was still six months away but by the look of Haversham's spreadsheet, over twenty people had already signed up and paid. And there were a lot of important people attending, if the footnote in the staff document was anything to go by.

Underneath the staff instructions was a single sentence warning of immediate dismissal without pay if they were caught taking photos. A spiel about protecting the community's privacy at events was dotted around the edges like a less than fancy border. Annie wondered what she'd have to do to blag herself an invite.

"Nice place for a party," Annie said, shrugging.

"Yeah." Swift closed the tabs and sent the computer to sleep. "Not my idea of a good time, though."

"What do you mean?" Annie asked, heading back to the door. "Too posh?"

Swift opened his mouth to answer when the door burst open and Mrs Haversham tottered in, flaked mascara under her eyes giving her the look of someone who had just returned from a good party herself.

"What on earth are you doing in here?" she screeched.

Swift pulled forwards and shook her hand.

"Mrs Haversham," he said, politely. "We're just waiting for your husband, he asked us in for a meeting in his office. The door was open, we hope you don't mind."

Annie nodded gently, going along with the ploy and hoping that Mrs Haversham was too drunk to notice they were lying.

"I'm sure he meant his Headmaster's office," Mrs

Haversham said with a grimace, ushering them out of the room. "No-one is allowed in here, not even me."

She tapped the side of her nose and staggered off towards the internal door between her house and the school. Annie and Swift followed close behind. As Mrs Haversham pulled at the thick, dirty brass handle on the door an almighty scream filled the air.

She faltered, turning back to Annie and Swift, the colour draining from her alcohol flushed face.

"Florence?" she stuttered, throwing the door open and breaking into a run in the direction the scream had come from.

Annie fell into a run after her as another scream filled the entrance hall of the school, echoing around the marble. Mrs Haversham's heels clacked along the floor, scraping as her ankles swayed sickeningly close to buckling in on themselves. Annie grabbed her elbow and helped her up the stairs.

"It's Florence." She was sobbing now, the crusty mascara running down to her chin. "It's my daughter."

They all hurried up the stairs and through the fire doors to the dorm rooms, the screams getting louder. Annie's neck was creeping with goosebumps as they rounded the open door and took in what greeted them. Immediately, Swift's police instinct took over as he threw out his arms and stopped both Annie and Mrs Haversham entering the dorm room.

"Stay back," he yelled. "This may be a crime scene."

Mrs Haversham wrestled against his arm, wanting to get past to get to Florence who was curled up in a ball beneath the swinging body of Una.

"Annie!" Swift yelled. "Keep hold of Mrs H, I need to check Una."

Annie did as she was told, working automatically and trying not to look at the way Una's ice blue eyes were bulging out of her head, no longer ice blue but a deep shade of blood red. Mrs Haversham was strong, fuelled no doubt by the adrenaline coursing through her body. But she wasn't the only one, and Annie threw herself around the woman and coaxed her back away from the dorm door and back into the hallway. Swift ignored Florence who was quite obviously, physically okay, and turned his attention to Una. With her mottled purple face and bulging eyes, the way her swollen tongue was lolling out of her mouth, too big to fit behind her bright blue lips, Annie knew they were too late to do anything to save her, but it was their duty to check and their duty to try even if it was futile.

He drew out a penknife and cut down the cord that was gripped so tightly around her neck the skin either side was puckered and bleeding. The light fitting swayed with the sudden release, and Swift lay the young woman as gently as he could on the threadbare carpet, pulling at the ligature with his fingers to release it.

"Call an ambulance," he yelled, as he started chest compressions, pumping so hard on Una's ribs that her arms moved with each thrust.

Annie had seen enough dead bodies in her time to know that Una was not rescuable. She also knew that unless a body was obviously deceased; a missing head maybe or already decomposed, that they were responsible for preservation of life until the ambulance arrived to take over. She withdrew her phone and dialled 999, all the while watching and feeling the fight drop from Mrs Haversham as she collapsed onto the carpeted floor in a heap that mirrored her daughter.

Swift shook his head, indicating to Annie what she already knew, but still he continued with thirty chest compressions followed by two breaths for what seemed like an age until the tell-tale static from a radio announced the arrival of the paramedics.

"We have a possible Cat 1," Swift said to the leading paramedic as she stepped past Annie and into the dorm. "Try not to disturb the scene if you can."

The paramedic knelt down next to the prone body of Una where Swift was still carrying out CPR though his arms must have tired as his compressions were less forceful than they had been. She placed a gloved hand on Swift's shoulder and shook her head, before unzipping her large, green bag and strapping electrodes to Una's bare chest. Swift knelt back on his haunches, his face red and sweaty. Annie felt useless, she wanted to go to him, to Florence, but she knew better than to step inside what could be a crime scene.

After a moment to catch his breath, Swift hauled himself up and went to Florence, helping her up from the floor and out to the corridor and her mother. But Florence shook him off, stepping to the side when Mrs Haversham lifted herself from the floor and tried to comfort her.

"Don't pretend to care," she sobbed at her mum, turning on her heels and starting towards the fire door. "You don't care about anyone except yourself."

"Florence," Swift yelled after her. "Wait, we need to talk to you, get a statement."

But the young girl didn't stop. She bashed through the door like a deer caught in the headlights and disappeared off into the school building.

"Do you want me to go after her?" Annie asked, turning to Swift who was already phoning it in.

"We've got a category one at Foxton's, send forensics." Swift ended the call. "Annie, no, this is more important."

He flashed his phone around the room, taking photographs as best he could as the paramedic started packing away. Stepping past the defibrillator, Swift knelt beside Una's body and lifted her right arm. Annie saw the flash go off.

"I'll need to cordon this room off," Swift said back on his feet and emptying out the room, he waited until the ambulance staff were through the fire door before getting his phone back out and swiping it unlocked. "Look at this."

He held it out to Annie who took it and brought it to her face, squinting at the picture to make out what Swift was showing her.

"Oh my god!" she said, and Swift nodded grimly.

The photo of Una's arm showed scratched writing dug into her skin, the same as Emily's. Only Una's words were different.

Love does not dishonour others.

SEVENTEEN

LILY

LILY SAT ON HER BED IN HER DORM, LISTENING TO THE *police chatter outside of her door. Their radios would occasionally crackle with talk from their control; state zero required, state six in attendance, officer required state 5 ETA, RTA all officers in the vicinity to report. It was all go, the noise was incessant. Lily had burrowed herself deep into her duvet and tried to block it out but all she could hear if she did that was the high-pitched scream that had pierced the silence earlier. She'd been hiding in her room, away from Mr Wells, when the screams had hit, though in some way, she'd been expecting it. Expecting something. But the chill she'd felt dragged her back to the night Emily died and the screams that had come from her own mouth. It had been enough to force her out of hiding and peek out of her door.*

Lily had heard the officers arrive at Una's room and had slid her door closed again. She'd known almost immediately why Florence was screaming, it didn't take a rocket scientist to work it out, though Lily wondered how long it would take the police. Two hours had passed since then and Lily had spent them lying on her bed staring at her ceiling hoping for a knock at her door. She wasn't going to volunteer the information, they'd have to ask her for it, and if they didn't even want to speak to Una's neighbour then on their heads be it.

Lily hadn't wanted to stay at Foxton's this holiday, Halloween was her favourite, and she had a costume all planned out. Sexy witch the label had read, and when the flimsy polyester outfit had arrived the next day via an harassed looking Amazon driver, Lily knew she was onto a winner. But her parents had decided to catch the ski season in Switzerland and her plans had been shot into flames faster than the stockings and cape had gone up when she'd torched it with a lighter. And now she was stuck here in her dorm, under a curfew that meant nothing because the teachers had absolutely no idea what was going on.

Then yesterday morning Lily had received that bloody letter and she was counting down the hours until school started back again, and she could rely on safety in numbers. The footfall outside the dorm door was trailing off, the sound of the radios quietening. Lily put down her phone and tiptoed back over to her door. She couldn't see anything useful out of the peephole, so she pulled her door open a crack and peaked out into the hallway. It was getting dark, the nights drawing in earlier and earlier making the already dull hallway glow with the florescent strip lights anytime someone moved. A few uniforms were milling around by Una's door and the unmistakable back of DI Swift was standing in the doorway next to the woman whose name Lily couldn't remember.

They backed out slowly, the uniforms making way too, and Lily's heart flipped right up into her throat, constricting her breathing as she watched a stretcher being wheeled out of the room. A zipped up black bag sat atop the trolley, a blanket laid over the top to somehow diminish the horror of what lay underneath, but it didn't. Not in Lily's mind, anyway. A wash of silent tears trickled down her cheeks as she watched them all leave through the fire doors, replaced by a team in blue overalls carrying large metal kits. They got to work quickly, and a lot more quietly than the police had, taping up the doorway and working in hushed whispers.

Lily slid on her slippers and made her way down to the other end of the corridor, towards the stairwell to the kitchen. She didn't want to walk past Una's room, she never wanted to see it again. The smell of vanilla and Gucci Red wafted down the corridor and gripped at Lily's insides like a claw. Una was still amongst them; Lily could practically hear her rasping laughter as she pushed open the door and headed down into the kitchen. A cool whip of air blew around her neck and made her skin prickle with goose bumps.

There was no-one around, the kitchen empty of people. Mostly the staff were given the holidays free too, given that the number of students left at the school was minimal and Mrs Haversham could mix up a batch of spaghetti bolognese in no time. Not that the sixth formers ate as a group, or at all if they were trying to look good for the guys who they'd preen themselves to see when they snuck out of their rooms at night and found their way to the city. Professor Haversham may rule the school with a steel fist, but he couldn't tell them what to do when it was out of hours. That was their feelings anyway.

Lily stole through the stainless steel and out into the school, hiding in the shadows of the large stairs in the entrance hall as the coroner headed up the procession of people carrying her friend out of Foxton's one final time.

Wiping her face with the back of her hand, Lily waited until they were all in the carpark before following them out. She slid around the side of the stone entrance, pulling her cardigan around her to protect her from the biting wind that had picked up since that morning. It was hard to believe that only a few short hours ago she'd been sitting under the tree wondering what to do about the letter she'd received. Una had shared hers, if she hadn't Lily may never have mentioned it. But this way, she wasn't to blame for not being there to protect Emily that night. She wasn't to know. That's what Lily kept telling herself. And now she needed to find Florence, she needed to know where she was.

There was one place she knew to look. Florence thought she was being so smart and discrete about her affair with Mr Wells, but you only needed to be in the same room as the two of them to feel the sparks flying and the tension thicken. Lily watched as Una was loaded into the back of an unmarked ambulance, crossed herself, and headed back around to the playing fields.

Her feet trampled a path across the damp grass, past the bandstand, and into the woods. The night drew in further here, the light dampened out by the autumnal trees. The smell of wet leaves and bonfires filled the air, an oppressive rag over her lungs. Lily breathed through her mouth; little shallow breaths that puffed white as though she was smoking. She stopped when she reached Emily's tree, distracted on her quest to find Florence by something tucked away at the thick base. Someone had left a single flower, a single white lily. Lily's arms prickled with a fear that blazed white hot and ran up her neck and over her scalp like tiny little creatures with many legs. She tried to shake it off, telling herself that it was a coincidence, nothing to do with her at all. Lily was the flower of death, of remembrance. But the eerie glow of the flower in the near dark made her stumble and trip in her haste to get past it to Mr Wells' cottage.

She hit the soft, wet moss with a thud, knocking the wind clean out of her lungs. Her eyes glanced around, not wanting to see past the darkness for fear of what might be there. Her heart thumped in her ears, but over the noise of her fear came a real noise. A crunch of feet through the undergrowth, the rustle of branches and brambles being pushed out of the way. She held her breath and clutched her knees into her chest, screwing her eyes tightly shut until a hand touched her shoulder and made her bladder loosen.

"Lily?"

Her eyes flashed open, recognition jolting her from her panic.

"Mr Wells!"

"Miss Parker, what on earth are you doing out here?"

Lily felt stupid, all curled up on the floor by the tree. She slowly unfurled herself and stood upright, her eyes still cast toward the dirt floor. Mr Wells took a step towards her, reaching out his arms, but Lily stepped away. Scared.

"Are you okay? What are you doing out in the woods at this time?" Mr Wells, stepped back, his hands raised in acknowledgement of Lily's unease.

"I could ask the same of you," she quipped back, angry at him for making her so scared. "They've found Una," she added, quietly, feeling the weight of her dead friend on her shoulders.

He dropped his head and puffed out a lungful of air.

"I heard," Mr Wells replied, kicking his toe at a lump of scrub.

"I was just coming to find Florence," she said, catching his eye.

His face flushed so bright that even in the darkness of the trees and the setting sun, Lily could see it light up his cheeks.

"I wondered if she might be out here, you know," she shrugged, not wanting to state the obvious, and leaving it ambiguous enough to not have to.

Mr Wells' face sagged, his previously attractive boyish looks hiding under the weight of newly heavy bags and deeply etched frown lines.

"I'm not sure where she is," he said, his eyes darting towards his cottage. "Best you get back to your dorm though, Lily. It's late."

He breathed another sigh and trudged on towards his home. Lily stood from the tree base and brushed herself down, watching her teacher as he unlocked his door and headed inside without a look back over his rounded shoulders. He was right, though. She needed to get back to her room, to the safety of the school. Florence would have to wait. But to Lily's surprise, when she emerged out of the blanket of trees, she heard others out on the school field. Voices tinged with excitement flooded the late night quiet. On the field in front of the bandstand stood the rest of the summer boarders, there were only a handful of them, but they were making a god-awful racket.

"What's going on?" she asked one of the younger girls she recognised from assembly.

The girl looked at Lily with eyes so wide she could see herself reflected in them.

"Have you heard about Una?" the girl said, a smile creeping onto her lips. "It's awful, she's hung herself. They've just taken her body out of the dorms now, none of us could stand to be anywhere near the building. It's just too hard."

Lily's stomach turned with disgust, and she did little to hide her scowl. This wasn't a game. She could see the excitement in the young boarder's eyes, and the other girls had a buzz about them that came with the thrill of a catastrophe that didn't affect them personally. They'd known of Una and Emily, they'd boarded together for a couple of years, but they were younger and had their own friendship group.

"Get a grip," Lily hawked, before storming through the gaggle of girls towards the school building.

Lily wasn't going to feign melodrama just to feel important. Emily had been her friend. Her best friend, and now she was dead. And Una was gone too, it was just too much to bear, but who could she talk to when the school was run by monsters, and her parents were probably halfway down a black run caring little about what their daughter was up to?

She stopped short of the stone steps and watched from the corners as DI Swift and his partner got into their car. Only when they had reached the tip of the driveway did she come out from her hiding place. Sneaking past Professor and Mrs Haversham who were having a heated argument in the doorway to their private home, Lily darted up the stairs and back into her dorm. Making sure the door was locked securely, Lily flopped down onto her bed exhausted. As she was falling into a dreamless sleep, she wondered why Mr Wells had been out in the woods this late at night and without a coat, but the thoughts weren't enough to stop her from drifting off.

What felt like seconds later a loud knock came at the door and brought her back to her dorm room with a startle. She muttered a few choice swearwords under her breath and climbed out of the covers. There was no sign of anyone through her peephole, so Lily opened the door just a crack, and peered out into the corridor at the person who'd knocked, holding her bare foot along the back of the door just in case.

"Hello," she said, looking around and noticing too late, as the door was forced open and Lily was sent flying back into her room, the skin on her foot still stuck to the draft excluder nailed to the bottom of the door.

EIGHTEEN

DAY FOUR

AFTER WHAT FELT LIKE A BLINK OF A SLEEP, ANNIE was back in the station nursing a large double shot latte with a doughnut and trying not to feel like a walking cliche. Tink was looking sprightly in a trench coat that would look more at home on a catwalk than a stale incident room. And Page was hammering away at his laptop as though he definitely got a full eight hours sleep last night. Swift was nowhere to be seen, despite telling Annie he'd see her here at eight on the dot. The tabletop looked like a comfortable place to lay her head, but the door bashed open just as Annie was rummaging in her bag for a cardigan to use as a pillow.

"Team," Swift said, looking way too sprightly himself to have had as little sleep as Annie. "Gather round."

"Morning, Guv," Tink winked. "We're already *gathered*."

Page shut his laptop lid and looked up as Swift made his way around the table and stood at the head of the room. The noticeboard behind him was getting fuller, a large picture of Una had been added, along with two boys who Annie assumed were the boyfriends of Emily that Una had told them about: Dan Barker and Stuart Hanover. They sat alongside Levi Wells, Professor and Mrs Haversham, and Emily's parents as possible suspects.

"Boyfriends, Tink?" Swift said over the table as Annie finished up her coffee and tried to sit upright.

"Well," she said, a twinkle in her eye. "Only the one right now, but you never know."

She winked again and a pale flush rose up Swift's cheeks.

"Not you!" he stuttered. "*Emily's* boyfriends. Florence said there were two of them, and Una told us *she* was kind of seeing one as well. Maybe there was something going on between them all. I've heard you females can be quote ferocious when it comes to marking your territory!"

Annie scoffed.

"Someone is pissing all over you at the moment, then Guv," Tink said, and Swift's face turned full blown gasket blowing colour.

But before he could quantify a comeback Tink was talking again.

"Dan Barker," she said, getting up and joining Swift, pointing at the picture of the younger looking boy. His curtained hair and shirt over long-sleeved t-shirt made

Annie think of a nineties soap character. "He was having sexual relations with Emily and sending the obligatory dick pics to Una too."

"Nice!" Annie whispered under her breath.

"Yup," Tink agreed. "Right piece of work. He's a local mechanic, works at a garage just up the road from the school. He's on his way in for questioning and should be here pretty soon."

"And the other one?" Swift asked, tapping his finger on the photo next to the pretty boy mechanic, a meeker, older looking guy with a shaved head and massive beard.

"Stuart Hanover," Tink said. "A butcher. He was at home with his granny the whole evening of Emily's death and we're checking yesterday's footage as we speak. She's got advanced dementia and so they have internal cameras to check up on the carers while Stuart's out the house. Time and date verified, he only got up to go for a wee and to scratch his arse by the looks of it."

"Marvellous," Swift said, patting Tink on the shoulder as she went back to her seat. "Page?"

DC Tom Page flicked open his laptop again and plugged in the cable next to him. His screen flashed up on the wall next to the blue noticeboard.

"Page!" Swift said, his eyebrows raised. "You've gone all high tech on me!"

"Nothing but the best," Page said, smirking. He clicked a few keys and a webpage filled the space, an archived newspaper article. "Here we have the connection between the Langtons and the Havershams."

Page whipped out a pointer and a red dot appeared

on the projected page on the wall. It zipped around a bit, as though Page was playing party games with a cat, until it settled on a small picture of four well-dressed adults holding glasses of Champagne. "Here they all are, twenty years ago now, back in London."

The headline read *Four Friends Join Forces,* but Annie's eyes weren't young enough to read the rest of the article. Luckily, Page was there to fill them in.

"The business was under a nondescript company name," he continued, waving the red dot around the highlighted quote on the article. *"We've found likeminded people and we want to engage with them."* The quote was as blinkered as the headline. "I checked Companies House and the four of them parted ways when the Havershams took over Foxton's, but the Havershams formed another company separate from Foxton's. It's called Plentiful Ltd. I found their webpage with a little help from the tech guys, which is weird in itself as normally businesses are flogging their wares not hiding them away so much; they need a team of IT experts to find them."

"What was on the webpage?" Swift asked, his hand rubbing his stubble.

"Nothing really!" said Page, his eyebrows raised. "Just a homepage with an abstract picture of a bull on it and a page all about their summer party. Maybe it's the Mrs, she's bored and is working a side hustle as a party planner."

"Like this?" Swift said, taking out his phone and showing Page the photograph he'd taken of the documents on Haversham's private computer.

Page nodded. "Yeah, pretty much. Look."

He tapped away at his laptop and the Plentiful page flashed on the screen, taking the place of the newspaper archive. The cursor clicked on the three lines at the top of the page and opened up the party planning. Annie recognised some of the items she'd seen on the Haversham's computer, but the price tag at the bottom of the page made her eyes water.

"That's some party!" she said, shaking her head at how the rich could charge whatever they like because their friends would all pay it.

The door to the incident room burst open and their DCI barged in, bringing with him the scent of Dupe aftershave that went out of fashion in the nineties.

"There's a young man in interview room two for you, Swift," he said, his large chin wobbling under his collar. "I wanted to see how you're getting on with this, should be an open and shut case."

He glanced at the projection and turned the same purple as his shirt.

"There's nothing open and shut about this case, Chief," Tink said, but was cut short by Strickland marching over to Page's laptop and slamming the lid shut.

"What's going on here?" he yelled, his chins now wobbling out of control. "Two dead girls and you're all here huddled around the Haversham's private business? GET TO WORK or you'll all be on traffic duty before you can scream my name."

He tried to turn to leave but his protruding stomach got caught between the table and the open door, so his angry exit was less dramatic than he was probably hoping. In fact, it was all Annie could do to hold in her laugh until the door was firmly shut behind him.

"What the hell was that?" Page said, gingerly lifting his laptop lid and powering up the projector again.

"O'Malley." Swift turned to Annie, his hands on the table. "Do you have a copy or photo anywhere of the spreadsheet from the Haversham's computer?"

"The one with the initials?" she asked, grabbing her phone from the table and swiping it open as Swift nodded.

"I think so." She tapped to her photos and handed her phone to Swift. "Don't swipe through them."

Swift raised an eyebrow at Annie and squinted at the screen. "I think we need to look deeper into these parties," he said, showing Annie her phone screen. He'd zoomed in on the initials which she could quite clearly see through the lines of the photo said RS. Now there could be a million and one people in the county with the initials RS, but Annie knew of one in particular, one who had just stormed their incident room. Robert Strickland.

"Call dispatch," Swift said to Page. "Get them to bring in Levi Wells. He said he worked at these parties."

Page left the room, dialling as he went. Annie picked up the photocopy of the letter Emily had sent to her best friends. "I wonder if the party had anything to do with the secret Emily wanted to share with her friends?"

"What kind of racket are the Havershams running through a girl's boarding school that requires a dark web website, has powerful people attending, and is more secretive than my Nan's marmalade recipe?" Swift said, tapping the pictures of the Havershams with his finger. "I think we need to talk to Florence and Lily here at the station too. Let's bring them all in. Annie, with me, let's go and see what Emily's rat of a boyfriend has to say for himself."

Dan Barker looked like a poor man's catalogue model, with the confidence of a Calvin Klein one. The way his legs were splayed out either side of the chair, his arms casually folded over his stomach, the flop of hair over his dark eyes, Annie knew they were in for a tough ride with this one.

"Officers," Dan said, tilting his chin as a greeting.

"Shut up!" Swift shouted, obviously getting the lay of the land as well as Annie. "I'm DI Swift and this is Ms O'Malley. We're not officers."

Swift took the chair nearest the windowless wall and left the one near the door for Annie. As she sat down, she looked closely for any signs of this young man's confidence being a cloak for shyness, anxiety, anything that ruled out him just being a massive dick, but she found none.

"You were the last person to see Emily alive," Swift said, his words as clipped as his movements. "Tell us what happened?"

Dan took his time, unfolding his arms and leaning forward into the table. Annie could see what the young girls saw in him, the confidence and the face combined was a deadly mix. Maybe literally.

"I wasn't the last person to see Emily alive, DI Swift," Dan said, slowly. "Her killer was."

Annie saw Swift's shoulders tense.

"Tell us about that night, Dan," she said.

A smirk grew across his face and Annie wanted to lean over the table and punch it clean off.

"We'd been in the woods," Dan started, leaning back and crossing one ankle over his knee. "It was cold, though, and Emily was in a weird mood. She wasn't her usual, welcoming self, you know? But we had sex anyway, it was over pretty quickly because I had to get back. So, I left her to walk back to school and she was very much alive when I did."

"You left her to walk back by herself?" Annie asked.

Dan shrugged. "She always did. Sometimes Stu would walk her back, but I didn't like getting too close to the school, you know. People talk."

"Stu, being Stuart Hanover?" Swift asked, and Dan nodded.

"She was sleeping with Stu too," he said. "I welcomed it, meant I wasn't trapped in a relationship, and I think these girls need to have a bit of a life outside of that school, you know. Emily and I weren't a steady couple, you know?"

"We guessed that from the fact you were sending pictures of your penis to Una." Annie could barely look at the smile on Dan's face.

"And I'd say, judging from those pictures, you've got little to be cocky about," Swift added. "So wipe that smile off your face and tell us what Emily was worried about."

Dan shuffled in his seat, his smile waning slightly, his legs closing a little.

"I don't know," he whined. "She was just being

weird. Offish, you know. Like she had other things on her mind."

"And you asked her what was wrong?" Annie asked, already knowing the answer as Dan shook his head. "Of course you didn't."

"Look!" Dan said, his eyes darting between Annie and Swift, his greasy forehead as slick as an oil spill. "I liked Emily, you know. She was a good girl. But it's not my fault she's dead. If you ask me, it's her weird head-teacher you need to talk to, not me. I gave Emily a good time, all he ever did was shout and scream and lock his own daughter away in her room."

Annie flinched. She'd known Professor Haversham wasn't a nice man, but she hadn't pegged him as an abuser. Why was he locking Florence up? Why did he need her out of the way?

"We're done with you, you little scrote," Swift said, getting to his feet. "But don't go too far. And try to pull your head out your arse, you could do with learning a thing or two about respect."

He swung open the door to the interview room and gave the uniformed officer at the door the nod. Dan Barker slunk away with the officer, his tail between his legs, and Swift took his place opposite Annie.

"O'Malley," he said, running his hands through his hair. "I don't like this; I think we need to get whatever information we can out of Levi Wells about the Haver-shams and bring in Professor Haversham too. On the quiet though, or the DCI will have us locked up and he'll throw away the key."

Annie nodded, about to agree when the door to the

interview room squeaked open and Tink stuck her head in.

"Sir," she said, her face drawn. "It's Wells, sir. He's gone missing."

"What?" Swift barked, shooting up from his chair.

Tink nodded. "And worse than that, so has Lily."

NINETEEN

"Get uniform out there, ASAP," Swift said, following Tink back to the open plan office. Annie quick stepped behind them both. "What do you mean he's *missing?*"

Tink gave a nod to Page who was at his desk, phone in hand, fingers poised over the keypad. He dialled and was talking within seconds. She spun to Swift and Annie.

"Uniform went to bring him in, as you asked," she said, perching on the desk nearest to her, much to the disgust of the officer trying to work there. "But when they got to his cottage they found it empty, no sign of him but sign of a struggle and his wardrobe had been cleared."

"And what did Haversham have to say about it?" Swift asked.

"And what about Lily?" Annie asked at the same time.

Tink looked between them. "Lily is assumed to be with him."

"What?" Annie didn't believe it.

"That's what Mrs H said." Tink shrugged.

"I don't like this," Annie said. "Has anyone spoken to Florence? Is she safe?"

"Mrs H confirmed Florence was fine, she's safe." Tink's eyebrows were heavy over her bright blue eyes.

"Let's head back to Foxton's now," Swift said. "Page, Tink, can you round up the uniforms and meet us there. O'Malley, I'll drive this time, I'd like to be able to feel my feet when we get there."

FORTY MINUTES LATER, SWIFT TURNED OFF THE main road and raced down the windy lanes to the driveway of Foxton's. The flashing blue lights of the cruiser illuminated the way through the dull afternoon sun, two uniformed officers greeted them as they jumped down from the car.

"Sir," one of them said, addressing Swift.

"Are you the officers who reported Wells as missing?" Swift said, reaching into the back seat to grab his coat as a fine drizzle started falling around them.

The officer nodded. "The cottage is cordoned off, we're waiting for forensics."

"Good, well done." Swift pulled his coat on and tugged the collar around his neck. "I'm now the SIO so any findings report straight to me."

"Sir." The officers said in unison.

"Get me some uniform out to the nearest train stations and check the local taxis to see if anyone had picked up a Levi Wells in the last 24 hours."

The officers took command and clicked at their

radios. Swift looked at Annie. "Cottage or school?" he asked.

"Cottage," she replied, and they started around the side of the school to the woods.

The walk seemed harder than it had done the previous day. The mulch underfoot slippier, the brambles thicker. Annie felt a sickness deep in the pit of her stomach as she grabbed hold of a trunk of a dappled fruit tree to stop herself sliding to the floor. Shivering, Annie pushed upright again and trudged on behind Swift. He heard her squelching and looked back.

"Are you okay?" he asked, concern flashing across his face.

She nodded and tried to smile, pulling back her shoulders. "I can't help thinking we're missing something here," she said, the pieces of the case rattling round her brain as she tried to order them.

"I know what you mean." Swift slowed to walk in line with Annie, brushing against her arm with his as they avoided the brambles either side of the path. "The parties, the headmaster, his alcoholic wife, the teacher/student relationship. It's as though this school is breaking every rule going yet doing it so well we've nothing to hold them on."

"Two dead girls," Annie said, quietly.

"Two dead girls." Swift stopped at the tree.

He stepped up on the roots that had twisted over each other and grown back out of the ground. Annie put a hand on the soft bark, it felt warm and smooth under her fingers. The thick branch from where Emily's lifeless body had been cut down was standing proud over the pathway, and through the dappled trees Annie could see the cottage. It's windows black.

"Do you think Lily could be with Levi?" Swift asked her.

"You're asking if Levi is the one who killed Emily and Una?" Annie said, walking around the back of the tree, carefully stepping over its gnarled roots that looked like fingers breaking out of the earth. "I can't see it. Yes, he's had a difficult upbringing, completely unorthodox and the Havershams have boasted about their good will but actually created a prison for him. But killing? I don't know."

"He has the opportunity," Swift said, pointing through the trees to the cottage. "The means, and possibly the motive if Emily's secret was about Florence and his relationship."

Annie nodded.

"But your Spidey senses are saying otherwise, yep?"

Annie nodded again, her brain whirring with the possible outcomes in her head. They had a school full of young girls, a family running it who plan private parties every summer that seemed to fund the boarders, and teachers sleeping with students. It was all wrong. All of it.

Swift looked grimly on as Annie pulled some gloves from her bag and strapped them over her hands, tugging her hair up into a ponytail to stop any stray hairs falling on a live crime scene. A patrol officer lifted the tape for them and grunted a greeting. It can't be easy being the officer in charge of protecting a scene, especially out in the cold October rain.

Inside the cottage felt damp and cold, as though Levi Wells had left weeks ago, not just hours. Annie knew this wasn't possible, they were here two days ago, and the cottage then was warm and loved, but she pulled her coat around her to stave off the chill that seemed to be seeping out of the walls. Her hair felt damp, the little baby tufts that normally sprung out in all directions from her forehead were plastered down with the low-lying mist that had encroached through the woods and into the cottage.

The tiny hallway felt crowded with both Annie and Swift in their heavy coats, so Annie pushed open the door to the living space they had sat in earlier in the week. Without the cosy fire it looked dark and dank. The carpet was in need of a good hoover with a topcoat of dirt and grime that took away some of the shine of the cottagey pattern.

"Anything?" Swift said from the hallway.

"Nothing jumping out at me." Apart from the dirty carpet, the room looked much the same as it had done. Though the coffee table was empty and there were no signs of any females living here.

"Same in the kitchen." Annie followed Swift's voice back out to the hallway and saw the small mishmash of kitchen through the low door. It was the epitome of a galley kitchen, and Swift's bulk took up what free space there was up to the door of the bathroom right at the very end. He pushed it open and stuck his head inside.

Annie could see the sink was clear of dishes, in fact all the surfaces looked clear of dishes but now there was a faint lemony smell mingled with the damp air.

"You getting that?" Swift asked, his eyebrow raised, leaning back out of the bathroom.

Annie nodded and Swift retraced his steps back out to the hallway.

"Someone has been cleaning?" she said, then turned to the narrow stairs. "Shall we?"

"Mmhmm," Swift hummed.

Annie took the stairs carefully; the rail was no longer really attached to the wall and the stairs were a ratio that builders were no longer allowed to use when it came to health and safety. Each tread was so narrow that the carpet thread barely had a chance to bend around before it was hanging down the next step. Bracing the cold cottage walls with both hands, Annie made it safely to the top and unlatched the bedroom door. It was just the one room, the cottage was smaller upstairs than down, which was crazy seeing as downstairs was already mouse house size. The door creaked warily, sending a shiver up Annie's spine as she pushed it open where she stood. Something stopped her following the door into the open room, the cold blast of air that had hit her face when the door swung gently open, or the mingling scent of rusty iron that followed it.

"Can we move off the stairs, please?" Swift said behind her, jolting her out of her reverie. "I'm not feeling overly safe standing here without crampons and an ice axe."

Annie looked over her shoulder to Swift with both arms outstretched, bracing himself against the walls with white knuckles and a shimmer of sweat on his forehead.

"Sorry," she said, stepping out of his way and into the

bedroom as Swift ducked through the doorway behind her.

"What the hell happened in here?" he said, looking around.

Annie followed his eye line to the bed, unmade, the duvet a crumpled mess at the foot, the pillows askew. The imprint of a person was visible in the way the sheets were rucked and a smashed glass was scattered all over where the head would have been. Annie stepped forward; she could see where the glass had hit the rough plaster on the wall before dropping to the bed below. And there had been someone in the bed, because tiny speckles of blood, so small they were almost invisible, dotted the cream sheets like an abstract painting.

"Swift," Annie said, pointing to the blood.

"I see it," he said, grimly. "Where are forensics?"

He took two strides and was at the window, looking out to the woods.

"Annie," he said, quietly. 'Come look."

Annie walked over and bent down to peer past the thick walls and the deeply inset window. Over the brambles and the low-lying mist, she could see the tree as clear as though it was in Levi Wells' back garden.

"Good view from bed," Annie said, looking back to the double bed facing the window. "Or a good vantage point to see someone on their own."

"You changing your mind about Levi?" Swift asked, straightening up.

"It's still open at the moment." Annie straightened up too, her back clicking with the movement.

Behind Swift, the only other furniture in the room,

was a tall boy chest that reached almost up to the low beams. Annie reached an arm and gently moved Swift to the side, sliding her body against his to get past him.

"O'Malley," Swift said, grinning. "I never knew you cared."

Annie felt her face flush and shot her head down, wishing she could take out her ponytail and hide behind her mass of hair. But there was something more urgent than her annoying habit of finding Swift attractive, and it was poking out from under the chest.

TWENTY

"What's that?" Swift asked, as Annie bent down to slide out the envelope from under the furniture.

She picked it up in her gloved fingers and looked at the front. It was a large cream envelope, much like the one Lily had received. Lifting the flap, Annie pulled out the letter inside:

Flossie, I have a secret. I know something that I shouldn't and I'm scared. I need to talk to you. I cant do it here. I can't do it over messages. I don't want anyone else to find out. I have to do it in person. Please meet me on Friday at the bandstand at 11pm.

Exx

"It's almost the same." Swift took the letter from Annie's proffered hand and she watched as his eyes scanned the page. "Let's get out of here and go and talk to Florence. Maybe she can shed some light on this letter or the secret. Maybe she got hers in time and knows something she's not telling us. Maybe she's covering for her boyfriend."

They exited carefully down the stairs and back out to the waiting uniform. Annie peeled off her gloves and threw them in her bag, waiting as Swift spoke urgently to the officer, his hands gesticulating his annoyance, probably at the wait for forensics. She took the path she knew well now and headed back to the tree to wait for Swift, not wanting the poor young recruit to have an audience to their berating. It wasn't his fault that Evans and his pink hair hadn't turned up yet, he was just guarding the scene.

The night was drawing in, casting the mist into a swirl of black fog underfoot. Annie treaded carefully, not wanting to end up on her knees in the wet mulch from tripping over a hidden tree root. She stopped and leant again the tree to wait for Swift, listening to the wind whip through the branches and the patter of the ever-present rain. A bird took flight, startling Annie as her heart hammered and her breath caught in her throat. She saw it, a large crow flapping its wings hard to take flight into the dusky sky before it caught a stream and started gliding gracefully away. With her eyes cast up, she saw the branch hanging out over the path, high above her head, the green lichen worn away where the rope had been tied. Her skin crawled with goosebumps and she rubbed her arms through her coat sleeves.

A rustle came from through the trees, towards the

school. A crack of a twig underfoot. Annie pushed herself upright from the tree and listened, her breath held, the pumping of blood loud in her ears. There it was again. There was someone else in the woods with them. With Annie.

"Hello?" she called, not wanting to stand here doing nothing, and not wanting whoever it was watching her through the trees to think she was scared. But she was scared, so scared that her hands had broken out into a slick sweat despite being freezing. Wiping them down her jeans, Annie called out again. "Is there someone there?"

A flurry of noise came from the direction of the watcher, as though a murder of crows was gathering for flight and not a lone bird.

"Wait," Annie shouted, starting to run after them, but she could barely see through the trees now, the sun had almost disappeared for the day. "Please."

The noise faded away and Annie was once again left alone with the wind and the rustle of the trees, her heart hammering so hard it was pounding up through her neck and trying to escape out of her mouth. The screaming noise of her phone ringing stopped her heart for a millisecond and Annie swore into the night as she rummaged around in her bag to find the source of the noise.

"Yes," she yelled into the phone as she tapped to answer the call.

"Bad time?" It was Tink. "Sorry. I couldn't get hold of Guv, so I thought I'd call you instead. I've got some news."

"Sorry, Tink," Annie said, letting out a long breath. "Sorry, no, I'm in the woods and I was just creeping myself out a bit. Swift is giving a young officer a piece of his mind about forensics; he's probably shouting too loud to hear his phone."

The chance to joke a little made the descending darkness slightly easier to deal with.

"Oy, I heard that," Swift said, coming through the undergrowth to the tree where Annie stood.

"It's Tink," she said to Swift, going back to her phone. "Go on Tink. You said you had news."

"Yeah," Tink replied. "Evans has just finished up with Una, he's on his way to the cottage now."

Annie relayed the news to Swift.

"Same drug found in Una's system," Tink continued. "And the writing was cut by the same hand, from what he can garner. He's ordered a specialist in handwriting to look at both samples, but even my untrained eye can tell it's very similar."

"So, we're looking at the same killer?" Annie asked. "Any traces?"

Tink carried on. "No, nothing that we wouldn't expect to be there. And Una hadn't had sex and there is no sign of sexual assault this time."

"So, they're probably not sexually motivated killings then?"

"Doesn't look like it. But it does look like someone she knew." Tink sighed. "There's no sign of a struggle, either on her body or in her dorm. She let in whoever it was, and she happily ingested whatever they drugged her with. Looks like it might have been vodka from the contents of her stomach. I'm heading home for the night now, see you guys in the morning."

"Thanks. Night Tink." Annie felt her heart sink. It was looking more and more likely to be the young teacher. An attractive man with power in a sea of vulnerable, impressionable young women. They may think they want to flirt with him, to get his attention, to be the one girl who can tempt him over from teacher to lover, but that was never going to end well.

"What's up?" Swift asked, his hand reaching out and stroking Annie's shoulder.

"Tink said the killer is someone Una knew," Annie said, as they started to walk out of the woods and back around to the school. "No traces of DNA that we didn't expect to be there. No signs of assault. The same drug used to sedate her and the same handwriting on the arm."

"So you're thinking it's looking more likely to be Levi and that's making you sad?" Swift was very astute when he wanted to be. "Why do you want him to be innocent?"

Annie stopped walking, sideswiped by the question. "I don't *want* him to be innocent," she said, wondering if that was true.

"But there's something in you that can't see him as the perp" This time it wasn't a question, and Annie knew it was the truth, even with the fingers all pointing at Levi Wells. "We've got more than enough to arrest him now; the Guv is taking it to the CPS as we speak, and we'll probably get a warrant before the day is up."

They broke out of the trees into the early evening darkness and Swift looked up towards the full moon. "Maybe before tomorrow is up," he said, glancing back down at Annie with a smile. "Let's go and find the Havershams."

Foxton's was deserted. The sounds of Annie and Swift's footsteps as they entered the grand hall echoed around the marble and wood. No lights illuminated the way. Not even the orange glow of a fire exit sign. Annie looked at Swift whose face was as scrunched up as hers was.

"Where is everyone?" she said in a whisper so as not to disturb the darkness.

Swift shrugged, taking the corridor that led to the Haversham's private residence. He knocked loudly on the locked door, unable to push it open.

"Maybe they're taking a few days out after everything that's happened?" Annie said, as they waited for someone to open the door.

"Maybe," Swift said. "Who's looking after the rest of the boarders then?"

"Maybe the handful of girls left here have been picked up by worried parents?" Annie scratched at the wood panelling with a fingernail.

"We'd know if they had." Swift shook his head and hammered again on the door. "Let's try the other one.

They half walked half ran back down the corridor and out down the stairs of Foxton's. The night sky was free of clouds which made the air icy cold and a sparkling of frost appear on the damp grass. They crunched across the gravel and onto the playing fields, the pavilion a dark blot on the landscape. Swift tried the handle of the

Haversham's private residence but there was no give. He knocked hard, his hand up to the glass.

"Police," he shouted. "We just want to check you're all safe. Can you let us in?"

There was no reply. Annie could see the flicker of light through the frosted glass of the door, as though there was a candle alight on the console table in the hallway. It made her think of Victorian homes lit by sconces on the walls and fires in their grates, gothic in their beauty and full of stories. Foxton's was full of its own stories and they were turning out to be Grimm Fairy Tales of their own making.

Annie moved around the building, even on tiptoes the windows of the other private rooms were all too high from the outside to see in. But the curtains were pulled on the office window and the kitchen lights were off by the looks of it, so they probably wouldn't have given up many secrets. A single light shone through the gap in what Annie thought was the dining room, but there was no way she could see in as the ground opened up in front of the house to a deep drop and a shingle path that probably was once the servants' entrance but was now completely blocked off. Avoiding a broken neck, Annie stepped back and tried to peer in from a distance instead, but there was nothing to see except the lining of a pair of very thick curtains.

"Nothing," Swift said, puffing out air. "And I tried to use a bit of force, but it's no good. I can break into new builds, but these old houses are like Fort Knox."

"What can we do?" Annie asked, watching Swift as he took out his phone and tapped.

"Bring in more cavalry," he said, and he started talking to whoever he had called. "Swift. We need a team with a ram at Foxton's. The family who lives here are missing, and we have reason to believe there is a killer on the premises who may wish them harm."

He barked a few more words and hung up, looking at Annie with tired eyes. His stubble had grown since that morning, scattering his chin with a dark shadow that made his eyes look darker and more intense. She cleared her throat and Swift shook his head.

"Sorry," he apologised. "I'm tired and hungry! The Rams are en-route, but they've got to go via the station as they have a perp with them. ETA an hour."

"An hour?" Annie said, her voice a little high pitched. "But..."

Swift shook his head. "I think Levi is long gone. I don't actually think he's an immediate threat. There are uniform here patrolling. Forensics are on their way and will go through the cottage with a fine-tooth comb. There's a BOLO out for Levi Wells and Lily Parker. And Florence is safe, so I feel as okay as I can about this whole mess for the minute. We can stand around here, waiting for The Rams to turn up or Evans to finish his job, or we can go and refuel and come back ready and raring to go."

Annie's stomach let out a giant rumble which answered Swift's question before she'd had a chance to even think about it.

TWENTY-ONE

They found a small, cosy looking pub halfway between Foxton's and the dual carriageway back to the city. Swift pulled the car into the carpark and they both trudged wearily to the door. Inside was an abundance of dark wood and cosy seating. Low ceilings striped with beams, walls dotted with faux candles and thick, dusty red curtains. The air smelt of spilt beer and fried chips. Annie's stomach let out another growl as a friendly looking waiter walked past them carrying plates so laden with fish and chips, they looked to be bending his wrists in the wrong direction.

"Take a seat wherever you like," he said to them. "It's order at the bar."

Swift walked to a table hidden at the back of the pub and pulled out the chair nearest the wall for Annie. She sat down and rested her elbows on the table, her face propped up in her hands, her exhaustion rising to the surface now she had taken the weight off her feet. Swift took the seat on the opposite side of the round table and handed Annie a menu. Her elbows gave a resistance as she peeled them from the table with a sticky sounding suction and took the wipe clean page from Swift. Scanning it, she quickly picked the fish herself, and battled half-heartedly with Swift as he stood to go to order and pay.

"Drink?" he asked, taking her menu and slotting it back into the wooden holder that also acted as their table number.

"Anything soft," Annie said, rubbing her face to try to wake up a bit. "We're on duty."

The corner of Swift's lips lifted in amusement and he headed to the bar, leaving Annie alone with her thoughts and a beer mat that was stuck to the table. She peeled it off with her fingernail and started tapping it against the table on its side, the way she always used to when she'd frequent old pubs with friends. Absentmindedly. It helped her think.

Glancing at Swift, she realised that her thinking wasn't all to do with the dead teenagers and the missing perp. She thought back to the ride in his car and the woman's coat in the back, the times he'd turned up late looking dishevelled, the time he was dropped at work. There was something going on in Swift's home life and she was itching to ask him what. But also, a little deflated at the thought his wife may have reappeared.

O'Malley, she admonished herself for thinking that, especially given the circumstances they were sitting together in this cosy pub. But she couldn't help the way she'd started to enjoy his company, the way he would bark at people he was annoyed with and square up to those who needed it, whist also offering her his coat because he noticed she was cold.

"Here you go," he said, and Annie blushed when she realised she'd been staring at him the whole time he'd been at the bar. "Thought you could use this."

He put down a small glass of what smelt like Malbec, along with a large bottle of sparkling water and a couple of tumblers replete with ice and lemon. Pouring them both a glass of water with a hiss and a glug, they fell into a comfortable silence. A clock ticked loudly in the background over the tinny muzak that was rattling the speaker over the bar, a gentle chatter played out amongst the other diners, soporific enough to make Annie's eyelids feel like lead.

"So, O'Malley," Swift said, startling Annie, she blinked hard and looked away from the flickering candle in the middle of the table to the man sitting opposite her. "What are you thinking?"

Annie blinked again, looking away, he really was attractive by candlelight. She hoped he couldn't read her mind as she'd been thinking once again about the return of his wife, the way Mrs Swift could just sweep in and out of his life as though the consequences were of little matter and his feelings even less.

"Erm," she said, taking a sip of water before picking up her wine and having a large glug. She tucked her hair behind her ears and felt them burning. "Well, I was just wondering how you were. You've been a bit distracted recently. Not your usual self. Not that I really know what your usual self is, of course. I mean I've only known you three months. But, you know, like there's something on your mind. And I was just wondering what that some-thing was."

Annie looked back again at her boss, his face impas-sive, but for the way his lips were almost smiling, his eyes crinkled with playfulness.

"Okaaay," he said, drawing out the vowel to make the word longer than needed. "That's good to know."

He took a sip of water, studying Annie with an inten-sity that made her stomach ripple over itself like the tide coming in.

"Not so distracted that it's taking your mind of your work, obviously." Annie was babbling now. "You're too professional for that."

This gained a laugh so hard from Swift that a few droplets of the water he'd just sipped ended up on Annie's hand. "Sorry," he said, leaning over the table and mopping it up with his own warm fingers. Annie's hand fizzed at the touch. "But me, professional? I think that may be the first time anyone has ever called me profes-sional. Thanks, O'Malley!"

He went silent for a moment and Annie had another swig of wine from the glass that she was grasping so hard in her sweaty hand it was liable to crack under the pres-sure. Just like she was about to.

"What I meant, though," Swift continued, the smile still bemused on his face. "Was *what are you thinking* in terms of the case?"

Annie felt the blood drain from her face, which was a good thing considering her cheeks had probably been the same colour as her Malbec. She rolled her eyes as Swift laughed again, softer this time, his hand now rested on the table just in front of hers, if she moved her fingers she could touch his. Instead, she drew her hand back and tucked it under her legs on the chair where no extra damage could be done. What was she thinking? They're in the middle of a horrible case and she'd been worrying about a non-relationship between her and her boss for crying out loud. She cleared her throat and was about to get into the deaths of Emily and Una when the waiter appeared and saved her.

"Two fish and chips," he said, putting their food down. "Enjoy. There's sauces on the table but let me know if you run out and I'll get some more sachets."

And with that he was gone, leaving behind the largest plate of fish Annie had seen in a long time. Swift grabbed some cutlery rolled in a red napkin and handed it to Annie. Thanking him, she took out the fork, and laid the paper napkin on her knee, flattening it down as it tried to roll itself back up again. She pronged some peas with her fork and nibbled, watching as Swift squeezed his lemon over the crispy batter and dug into his own dinner.

"Tell me what's going on in that head of yours?" Swift said, after a few minutes of quiet eating. "I'd like to know where you stand in this whole case."

Annie had just bitten into a large crispy chip covered in mayo, so she took her time over answering this question, careful not to make the same mistake as before. She swallowed and had a sip of water, looking around to check they weren't in earshot of anyone else.

"So what do we have?" she said, quietly, poking her fish with her fork. "When we look at the boiled down facts, we have two dead teens who were keeping a secret."

"What kind of secret?" Swift's hand was poised between his plate and his mouth, his own fork laden with ketchupy chips dotted with a few peas.

Annie thought for a moment while she had another mouthful of melt in the mouth cod with crispy buttery batter.

"A secret that was worth killing to keep," she said eventually. "So one that meant a life changing deal to someone out there."

"So we're looking at something illegal." Swift scooped up a forkful of peas into his mouth. "Say, like a teacher student relationship?"

The more she thought about it, the more Annie felt that all fingers were pointing to Levi Wells. The young, attractive teacher who had maybe led more than one of the girls astray. She nodded.

"He might have Lily," she conceded. "Though he is definitely in a relationship with Florence, there is nothing to make me think he is sleeping with any other students. But that's not to say he wouldn't go to extremes to cover up his relationship to keep it secret."

"And if he saw Florence's letter," Swift said. "And thought it was about his relationship with Florence, maybe that's why he decided to shut them up. He wouldn't just lose Florence; he'd lose his whole life. That's reason enough to stop the other girls talking. Like when he saw us talking to Lily in the common room? He practically marched her out of the room."

Annie remembered the confident way Levi had stood

his ground about Lily being underage. "Maybe he was scared she would spill his secret to us?"

"It all boils down to the secret, doesn't it?" Swift said. "When we know what it is, we know who killed Emily and Una."

"So where are we on the Havershams and Emily's parents?" Annie asked, putting down her cutlery on her empty plate. "Are they still on the radar?"

Swift nodded, mopping the last of the ketchup from his plate with a fat chip and sitting back in his chair contentedly. "We've got officers waiting for them to return home, then we're bringing in both parents for questioning and Florence will be looked after while they're away, see if we can get anything out of her too."

"About the parties?"

Swift nodded, picking up the menus from their block and handing one to Annie. She thought about resisting, but the urge for something sweet was too strong.

"I think these parties, the whole side business using Foxton's is underhand and dodgy," Swift said, his eyes scanning the laminated menu in his hand. "But we don't really have any answers about anything. And I'm sick of going round the houses. We need facts!"

Swift's phone chirruped in his pocket and he fished it out as Annie studied the dessert menu herself.

"Swift," he barked.

The silence that ensued made Annie forget the tiramisu and the jam roly-poly with custard and look up at Swift as he sat silently listening to whoever was on the other end of the phone.

"We'll be right there," he said, before ending the call

and throwing his phone on the table, ushering over a waiter with the flick of a hand and a sorry smile to Annie. "It's Levi Wells, he's been found. Apparently, he was hiding in the woods near the edge of the school grounds. They're holding him at Foxton's."

"And Lily?" Annie said, getting to her feet and draining the last of the wine from her glass, thinking about the noise she'd heard back in the woods and wondering if Levi had been about to come for her too.

Swift shook his head. "No sign."

They rushed out of the pub, waving their thanks to the bemused barman standing polishing a glass with a chequered tea towel, and straight to the car. Swift drove as though he hadn't just eaten his body weight in food, and Annie breathed out a crack in her window to stop hers from reappearing. Luckily the drive was short.

It was pitch black as they swerved back into the car park, the lights from the police blues switched off and only the headlights shone the way as Swift and Annie ran up the steps to the entrance hall and the answers that lay beyond.

TWENTY-TWO

"Levi Wells," Swift said, entering the classroom that had been earmarked as an interview space. Wells had been seated at a table just inside the door, so Annie and Swift took the seats opposite.

Wells bowed his head like a man who'd given up, but that wasn't enough to hide the black eye that was appearing like a rash, and the blood red lines scratched down his cheek. Annie felt her fish supper roll over in her stomach as though it was still in the ocean. Wells caught her looking and his handcuffed hands flew up to hide his cheek, automatically scratching his head, his eyes flashing between her and Swift. He was soaked through, his hair plastered to his head and his jumper was dripping. The smell of damp soil permeated the room.

"Levi Wells," Swift said again. "You have been read your rights and are under arrest, so I am going to record this conversation."

He took his phone from his pocket and sat it on the table, the voice recorder ticking up the seconds as it captured the ambient noise from the classroom. The silence punctuated by the rhythmic rain on the window was oppressive. Annie could feel the fear seeping out of Wells, the way he sat not moving, his arms up to protect his body, his knees jittering silently under the table. Swift leant forward on his chair, his face as close to Wells as he could manage.

"What happened to your face?" he said, nodding his stubbly chin in Wells' direction.

Wells wrapped his arms around his body even tighter.

"I told your officers," he said, his voice reedy. "I fell over."

"Onto someone's fist?" Annie couldn't help herself. "Those marks, they look like scratches. Fingernails maybe? Was someone trying to get away from you, Levi?"

Levi caught her eye and quickly looked away. He looked like a little boy lost. Annie wanted to hate him, but all she felt tugging at her heart was a sad sense of not belonging.

"Where's Lily Parker?" Swift was not messing around, and by the looks of him, he wasn't feeling sorry for the young teacher. "What have you done with her?"

"Nothing!" Wells' voice screeched, and he cleared his throat. "I haven't done anything to Lily. She's a good student. A nice girl."

"A girl is exactly what she is, Levi," Swift spat. "Nothing more than a girl. And we know how you like them, don't we?"

What blood was left in Wells' face drained completely away. Even his lips started to blend in with the pallor of his skin, tinted with scabs where he bit incessantly at them. He pulled his sleeves down over his handcuffs and down past his fingers and tucked his hands away completely in the fabric.

"It's... it's not like that." He knew he had lost, the edge to his voice, the hardness had all but been erased away. "With Florence. It's not like that."

Annie could see Swift going in for another blow and she got there first.

"What is it like then, Levi?" she said, softly. "Tell us."

Swift shuffled in his chair, and Annie reached a hand under the table and placed it firmly on his knee. He needed to calm down before Levi Wells shut off completely and put Lily in even more danger. She felt his leg tense with the touch and lifted her hand away.

Wells looked like he had the weight of the world on his shoulders. His sunken eyes searched the tabletop and eventually landed on Annie.

"It isn't like that," he said again. Annie nodded encouragingly. "Growing up, I used to look out for Florence. Mr and Mrs H said I would be doing them a favour, but really, they were all helping me. I enjoyed having another person to play with, to have responsibility for."

He looked down at his fingers, now uncovered, and Annie noticed again the lines of scarred skin. He saw her looking and the air left his body in a huff.

"I was so used to being tormented," he continued, lifting his hands for all to see. As his sleeve rolled back down his arms, Annie could see the scars continued on past his cuffs. "These scars were with me before I was taken into care, but the kids there used to love teasing me, and trying to add to them. They were red raw back then, courtesy of my mother, but they soon healed, as physical scars do. It was only when I found myself in a real, loving family that my mental scars began to heal too."

"The Havershams?" Annie asked, remembering their first conversation with Wells.

He nodded. "When they took me in, Florence was only four and she was a handful. But she took to me and I helped look after her."

He stopped and puffed out more air. "She grew to be a good friend, we never felt like family, not really."

Swift muttered something unrecognisable, but Annie pushed on.

"When did things change?" she asked.

"There are things you need to know about the Havershams." Levi looked up at Swift this time. "Things that maybe they wouldn't want getting out in the open. 'Not for everyone's eyes, Levi' they used to say to me. But I helped them out anyway."

"Are you talking about the parties?" Swift asked.

There was a slight nod to Levi's head. "They weren't parties to start with, just small gatherings. I'd serve drinks and the occasional line of coke on a bloody silver tray." He gave a guttural laugh that held no humour.

"Drugs?" Swift asked.

"Yeah," Levi went on. "Looking at some of them, I'm not surprised they needed drugs. It was like an orgy of aristocracy but without the money. They're so grotesquely indulgent these days, too. Urgh. Makes me sick just thinking about it."

A flicker of recognition fluttered in Annie's head. "Wait!" she said, interrupting Levi. "The parties are orgies?"

"Yeah," Levi said, as though she'd asked him something obvious. "Can't you tell by the terminology? Unicorns, bulls..."

Swift slammed his hands down on the table. "No! We're not those kinds of people!"

"Speak for yourself," Levi said, his face twisting into an ugly grin. "Your boss, Bob Strickland, is never one to turn down a key swap with Emily's parents. In fact, Mrs Langton used to get so irate with Emily for dropping her grades, she was worried that Professor Haversham would kick her out of their exclusive club."

Annie's eyebrows nearly hit the roof. So the initials on the spreadsheet were Strickland's. His insistence to keep things under wraps and dealt with quickly and quietly suddenly made a whole load of sense. Annie glanced at her partner whose ears had turned a nice shade of pink.

"Be careful what you say under caution," Swift said, nodding to his phone on the table.

"Oh, it's all true," Levi said, shrugging. "I keep their records, payments, stuff like that. I wouldn't lie about something like that."

"But you'd hide it from the world, the fact that the Havershams are using a *school* to carry out some sort of depraved sexual orgy?"

Levi spread his hands. "Look, it's not up to me to judge what is or isn't morally right, neither is it up to you, sir."

Annie couldn't help but notice how well-spoken this man was. He wasn't angry or shouting, he was simply stating facts.

"They're *children!*" Swift shouted, the antithesis of Levi.

Levi flinched, his whole body moving back to get away from Swift's shouts. His head started shaking backwards and forwards quicker and quicker.

"No!" he said, louder now. "No. You're mistaken."

"What, so teens are fair game now are they? What have they done with Lily and who silenced Emily and Una?"

Levi's eyes widened. "No. No, no. The girls have nothing to do with the parties. They're never there when they happen. It's always during the holidays and the remaining boarders are always sent away on trips. They're not depraved, Sir, they're just playing out middle aged fantasies."

That shut up both Annie and Swift. The ticking of the rain carried on at the window, tapping to be let in.

"So why are you wasting our time with them?" Swift looked as though he was going to blow a gasket.

"You asked me, Sir." Levi's shoulders were slumped again. "And they were when it started."

"When *what* started?" Annie asked, annoyance building in her as much as it was Swift now. There was a girl missing, and a whole family who couldn't be found. "What are you trying to tell us here, Levi?"

"I don't want to speak badly of the Havershams, they were good to me." Levi bit the edge of his thumb nail and pulled at a loose bit of skin there, blood spotting the edges. "But when she got older, I guess they thought she was in the way of their parties. So Florence would get put away somewhere safe until they were over."

"*Put away?*" Swift said, calmer now.

"Yes," Levi continued. "Mostly in the cupboard under the stairs. Their private stairs."

"Shit!"

"I know! I thought maybe it was because Florence would sneak down and interrupt, she has a habit of poking her nose in places she perhaps shouldn't. And she can ask difficult questions. But she's so caring and kind and she makes me feel like I'm the only other person on this planet when we're together. Like I don't need anyone else except her. I don't even have any social media or a mobile phone, because why would I need them when my whole world is right next to me? But, yeah, sorry, no matter how many difficult questions she asked, or how many times she snuck down to get a look at her father wrapped around other people, no one deserves that."

Annie's senses were crawling around in her head, somehow it felt odd. She kept quiet and listened as Levi continued talking about his relationship with Florence.

"She'd spend more and more time at mine, we talked for hours, she'd tell me all about her life and ask me about mine. I had dreams to go travelling when I had saved enough up from teaching, but she made me realise I didn't need to fly to the other side of the world to find happiness."

Levi ran his hands through his mop of hair, leaving it sticking up unruly and in need of a wash.

"But the older she got, the more she was locked away.

Little things would trigger it: coming home too late or a broken glass or plate. She'd be in there for hours at a time, and eventually she was drugged to make it easier to keep her quiet. I felt awful. I couldn't argue with them because they could have kicked me out and made sure I never saw Florence again. That would have been a fate worse than death. So when she came of age, I asked her to be my girlfriend and I told her parents that I'd look after her. They agreed. But there are some nights she wakes screaming, thinking she's back in that cupboard."

The room felt hot and stuffy, despite the burgeoning winter outside, and Levi had a sheen of sweat covering his flaccid face. He picked at his thumb nail with the fingers on the same hand, a nervous habit that was long in the making from the looks of the raw tissue around the nail bed.

"So you had no reason to keep your relationship a secret from her parents?" Annie asked.

Levi shook his head. "They know. But it could never get out further than family because of the damage it could do to the school reputation."

A little trickle of a thought was gathering in Annie's head. She couldn't quite mould it into a fully formed thing yet, but she had that itch that meant it wasn't far away. At least she hoped it wasn't, because it felt important.

"What did they drug her with?" Swift asked.

"I... I'm not a hundred percent sure," Levi stuttered. "I think it was sleeping pills, that's what I was told. Nothing that would hurt her. But I saw it happen on more than one occasion and it looked like a clear liquid dropped into hot milk, and that's not any sleeping pill I know of."

Annie looked at Swift who gave her a brief nod and pushed his chair back. Before he could terminate the interview, the door clicked open and Tink came into the room.

"Guv," she said, quietly. "Haversham's back, I'll tell him you want to speak to him next?"

Swift nodded.

"Does he have Florence with him?" Levi asked, his eyes wide now.

Tink looked at Swift who gave her a nod.

"No sign of Florence, not yet."

"What?" The whites of Levi's eyes burned red.

"Our officers are talking to him now, but it seems he's just been out for the day and Florence and her mum stayed at home." Tink retreated out the classroom.

"That's a good thing, isn't it, Levi?" Annie asked, noticing the aggravated change in Levi.

"No!" he shouted. "No, it's not."

"But Professor Haversham wasn't with Florence, and from what you've been telling us, that's probably a good thing. We knew he was strict; we just didn't know *how* strict." Swift tapped the back of his chair with his fingers. "We're going to bring him in and possibly press historical charges for what you've been telling us. But our priority now is to find Lily Parker."

Levi pushed his own seat back, it toppled over with a clatter that sent a uniformed officer running into the room and straight over to restrain him. The scared teacher held his hands up in surrender, backing away. With wide eyes he turned to Annie and Swift.

"Don't you get it?" He looked like a trapped animal. "She's in danger! If it's just the two of them alone, if it's just Florence and her mum, then *she's* in danger. You need to find her. And you need to find her before something bad happens, because I can't take another death. Please. Please go and find her."

TWENTY-THREE

Swift and Annie ran through the corridors and back outside into the freezing rain. Annie pulled her coat around her and lifted the collar against the biting wind as Swift went over to a group of uniforms, talking animatedly. The crackle of police radios and the flashing of the blue lights felt eerie against the backdrop of the large gothic building. The school had lost all of its glamour, all of its intrigue now Annie knew of what happened behind the thick walls. Swift had said he'd grown up knowing of the reputation of the school and she wondered what would happen to that now there were two dead students, and a history of abuse to go with them. A shudder ran right through her core as she thought of Florence and Lily and the fear they must be feeling now, wherever they may be. She hoped they were together and away from Mrs Haversham, and she hoped they were still alive.

"Uniforms are doing another sweep of the school and

grounds," Swift said as he crunched back over the gravel to Annie. "They're checking the Haversham's residence too, now Professor Haversham is back."

"What's he saying?" Annie asked, rubbing her arms to stay warm.

"Let's walk to stay warm," Swift said, leading Annie around the back of the school to the playing fields. "He's in denial. Apparently, he's been away all day at a head-teachers' conference and had no idea of what was unfolding here at Foxton's."

"He went to a headteachers' conference?" Annie was gobsmacked at how detached from reality Professor Haversham was.

"Yeah, he needed to keep up the front. His words."

They rounded the back of the grey building, following the strip of light illuminated from Swift's torch. The pavilion came into sight and a light came on in Annie's head.

"Swift," she said, upping her pace, the cold forgotten. "Shine me a light to the pavilion, would you?"

Before he could answer she was changing direction and heading away from the school towards the wooden structure. Something she'd seen was triggering a flash of an idea in her. Swift caught up, lighting the way, and Annie hoped that it would still be here, that her idea could come full circle.

"What's up?" Swift said as Annie climbed the slippery steps to the platform.

The light stopped midway over the rotten wood, so Annie drew out her own phone and illuminated the rest.

It was there, lying on its side just where they'd left it. Annie stooped to pick it up, the bottle cold even through her gloved hands.

"The vodka bottle?" Swift said, grabbing an evidence bag and holding it open for Annie.

Annie nodded, dropping the bottle inside. "It just came to me then; the vodka is the same brand as the shelves of it we saw in the Haversham's private residence. Grey Goose isn't affordable for students, is it? Why didn't I think of that when we saw it here the other day?"

"What are you thinking now?" Swift said, sealing the bag.

"What if Hetty Haversham was here that night?" Annie said, picking up the two glasses and waiting for new evidence bags. "What if she found Emily waiting for her friends? What if she somehow intercepted those letters and thought the secret Emily knew was about her? About how she locked her own daughter in a cupboard when she got too much? How she was drugging her? Because Rohypnol is a clear liquid isn't it? And that's what Levi saw."

Swift nodded and held open a bag for each glass. He sealed them up and radioed for a uniform to come and collect and record them. Annie stepped down from the platform, carefully treading on the steps so she didn't slip. She couldn't stand still and wait for the officer, not with the idea forming in her head. Something Levi had said back in the classroom was still worrying her, but she couldn't place it. As Swift spotted the torch beam of the police constable, and started towards them, Annie switched off her own phone torch and plunged herself into darkness. She paced; the only thing she could see was the breath clouding in front of her, everything else was blanketed in darkness as her eyes slowly became adjusted to the night.

What was it Levi had said? What was it that was almost there, in the periphery of her thoughts, trying to pull together to form a cohesive idea? She moved backwards and forwards, keeping the pavilion nearby so she didn't wonder too far. The grass had started to crisp up underfoot and the air was so fresh that it hollowed out her lungs with each breath. Back and forth, back and forth. And when Annie turned, her mind almost screaming at her to put together the pieces, she stopped. Distracted by a flicker of something in the distance. Squinting her eyes to get a better look, Annie felt her heart start to pound through her coat.

"Swift," she shouted, not turning back as she didn't want to lose eye contact with the light. "Swift, come here, quick."

Swift was by her side in an instant.

"Look," she said, lifting her hand to point. "There's a light up ahead. Can you see it?"

"Is this payback for the time we saw the fire through the trees?" he laughed, but Annie thumped his arm and tilted his jaw in the direction of the little dot, her hand sticking to the stubble on his chin.

"What's in that direction?" she cried. "Is it still part of the school grounds?"

The rain turned from light drizzle to heavy torrent, as

though someone had turned the tap all the way around. Annie pulled her hood up over her hair, listening to the noise of the water on the trees around them. She felt it seep into her shoes and stick her trousers to her skin in a matter of seconds. Then the clouds parted, and a flash of lightning lit everything up for a millisecond long enough to see the outline of the mobiles. A few seconds later a low rumble cut through the noise of the rain.

"Bloody hell," Swift growled, lifting his own hood and ducking against the rain.

"It's the mobiles, Swift," Annie said. "Come on."

She grabbed a soaking wet sleeve of his wax coat and started dragging him in the direction of the old temporary mobile units that were tucked around the back of the school. Another flash of lighting brightened the playing fields. About three seconds later came the thunder. Annie faltered; they were sitting ducks out here in an expanse of flat grass. Mostly she was thinking about the lighting, being burned from the inside out as a fork of electricity ran through her body from her hair. But the two of them were also out there alone, in the middle of the fields surrounded by the black windows of the school where any eyes could be watching them at any time. A shudder ran through Annie that was nothing to do with the angry rain that was coming down in torrents.

There's no one out here, Annie tried to tell herself, as she picked up her pace towards the mobiles. But there was, wasn't there? Mrs Haversham had Lily and Florence, and their lives were in danger.

The thunder crackled and fizzed louder than before

as the night sky lit up. The storm was right above their heads making the fields vibrate and the trees loom in like zombies with crooked limbs. Annie wiped the rain from her eyes with her free hand, but it was no good, she was soaked through and shivering. The glow of the light was a welcome sight though, now obviously a light from the prefab building block the furthest from the path. Swift grabbed his hand free and Annie only then realised she'd been holding on to it as they ran. He lifted his sodden hair from his forehead, sweeping it over and tucking it under his hood so it was out of his eyes. Drips of water fell from his nose and his chin and chucked down the arms of his wax jacket. He grabbed his phone and tried to swipe.

"Argh," he yelled, unzipping his coat and wiping the phone screen on his jumper. "It's too wet to work."

"What are you doing?" Annie yelled over the rain and the low rumble of thunder.

She could barely hear as he shouted back. "I need to call this in, we need to tell them where we're going." Swift gave an angry yell again and pocketed his phone. "It's too wet."

Annie turned back towards the window, not wanting to waste any time. When Levi had told them they needed to find Florence it wasn't just a request, it had come from his heart. He had been scared.

She's in danger! If it's just the two of them alone, then she's in danger.

What if they were too late? What if she had already done her worst?

The ground underneath Annie's boot slid out from

under her and she went down with a thud, her left leg landing awkwardly as she took her full weight on her ankle. Something popped and a sharp bolt of white-hot pain shot up her leg as she cried out.

"Are you okay?" Swift was right beside her, squatting down, his face close to hers, rain plummeting down it.

Annie nodded, pushing herself up from the mud and trying not to wince when her foot hit the floor. It hurt. But Annie was pretty sure it didn't hurt as much as being drugged and strung up by the neck. Leaning on Swift's arm they reached the steps of the mobile unit. The light through the window was timid, flickered intermittently, occasionally plunging them both into darkness. But they were too high off the ground to see in. Metal steps led to the door and Swift grabbed hold of the rails and crashed his way up to the top. Annie tried, putting one foot on the lowest step and pulling herself up with her arms because her other ankle felt like jelly. Jelly with razor blades sliced through it. She looked up at Swift who had his hand up against the window.

"Oh god." He breathed against the glass, steaming it up with his breath and rattling the door handle.

"What?" Annie yelled over the rain. "What is it? Who's there?"

Dragging herself up the rest of the stairs as Swift pushed open the heavy fire door, the lightning flashed so fiercely above that the crackle sent a fizz of static through Annie's scalp. Even from the tiny gap in the door, the blood on the floor was obvious. Annie's stomach rippled as she hauled herself in, the welcome respite from the rain marred completely by what was waiting for them inside the damp, freezing building.

And as she looked down at the body, Annie knew what it was that had been niggling away at her like a rat gnawing through a wire, and her whole body sank to the bloody floor.

TWENTY-FOUR

"Oh God!" Annie's hands flew up to her mouth, the pain in her ankle forgotten. "Swift, is she... is she still alive?"

Swift stumbled forwards, towards the body slumped in the corner of the mobile. Her head was slick, wet with blood that had pooled around her shoulders where she'd fallen, trailing thick lines down the white board still covered in algebra. An old desktop pencil sharpener lay on its side beside her, thick with congealed blood and what looked like hair. Annie felt her stomach turn over as Swift grabbed a pair of blue gloves from his pocket and dragged them over his fingers with difficulty. Annie wondered if Swift's hands were as cold and damp as hers felt. Icy with a fear that was dripping through her whole body.

A lone zippo lighter flickered a few feet from the body; lit and discarded. The red-hot flames licked close enough to the leg of a classroom chair to have blackened the metal and fill the room with an acrid smell that hit

Annie in the back of the throat. She swallowed twice to try and dislodge the ball of fear in her throat. It didn't work. With an open mouth, Annie moved to pick up the lighter and click it shut when another flash of lightning lit up the whole block and the body let out a keen that loosened Annie's stomach to an ice bath.

"Help..." The croaky voice sounded disjointed, as though it couldn't quite be coming from the same person. "Help... me."

"Swift!" Annie yelled over the rumble of thunder that shook the thin walls and the rain that hammered deafeningly on the flat roof.

"Call for backup," he yelled back, dropping to his knees to help.

Annie knew she could be wrong. But something had clicked inside her head as soon as she'd seen who was lying on the floor covered in blood. The more she thought about it, the surer she was that when Levi had sat in the interview room and cried for them to help, he hadn't been talking about Florence being in danger he'd been talking about her mother. The niggling feeling Annie had felt all the way through his interview had dropped perfectly like tumblers in a locked safe at the sight of Mrs Hetty Haversham.

"When they took me in, Florence was only four and she was a handful," He had said. *"I had dreams to go travelling when I had saved enough up from teaching, but she made me realise I didn't need to fly to the other side of the world to find happiness. I don't need anyone else except her."*

When he had been talking about Florence and his

feelings for her, it had seemed one sided, infatuation Annie had thought. The times Florence spoke of her parents, the anger and hatred that had oozed from her wasn't a result of the Haversham's strict ways with her, but the narrative Florence wanted other people to believe. Annie knew now that Florence wasn't the one at risk here, Florence was the danger. Reeling people in and taking what she wanted before spitting them out when she was done. From the outside, Florence was as sweet as pie, but underneath her pretty exterior was a hardened girl who wasn't afraid to kill.

Lily!

As Annie waited for her phone to connect, she limped across to Mrs Haversham, forgetting the flickering lighter, and bent down so her head was close to Hetty's blood crusted face.

"Where's Florence, Mrs Haversham?" she said, waving a hand to hush Swift before he got any words out. "What's she done with Lily?"

Through the dried, crusted blood, plastering her blond fringe to her forehead Annie saw Mrs Haversham's eyes roll back in her head. Swift gathered her up by the shoulders and felt around her head, presumably for the wound that had caused the flood of blood. From the colour of Mrs Haversham's face, Annie guessed that she'd been here for at least two hours, maybe more.

"Mrs Haversham." Annie tried again. "We know about Florence. You need to tell us where she is, she's got Lily and we think she's in danger."

Swift shot her a look, but Annie didn't care. This woman had been protecting her daughter for too long, through too much. Two girls had died, and Annie didn't want there to be a third. The call connected and Annie barked instructions into the mobile; ambulance needed, police already at the scene. She shouted the address as the rain drowned out her words and hung up the phone when the control room confirmed. Lightning brightened the room as Swift laid Mrs Haversham down on her side and into the recovery position. Her eyes flickered as wildly as the lighter flame; topped with the lightning flashes, it made Annie's spine tingle.

"Mrs Haversham, please?"

A croak. A rattling cough. Mrs Haversham spat out bloody phlegm onto the plastic tiles beneath her cheek. A bloody dribble hung from her lip, clinging to her face as it dripped to the floor.

"I tried to stop her." Her voice was thick with the hangover from her head wound. "I tried to lock her away. But she's evil."

Mrs Haversham's whole body rocked with the force of a cough. She groaned and more bright red phlegm fell from her mouth. Annie was assaulted by the stench of metallic rich vomit and she gagged, holding her sleeve over her nose and mouth as she tried to listen to what Mrs Haversham was saying. Swift grabbed his own phone from his pocket, wiping it dry on his trousers, he swiped and dialled. A crack of thunder overhead made Annie's head run cold. She listened to Swift give instructions to what must be the team already at the school before he looked over at her.

"They're on their way here to sit with Mrs Haversham and wait for the ambulance," he said, and turned his attention to their patient. "Hetty, you're going to be okay. Help is on the way now and an ambulance isn't far behind. You're going to be okay, just relax but try to stay awake."

Annie felt ashamed listening to how kind he was being when she'd gone in like a sledgehammer and blasted questions at her. But there was still a teenager in danger, and they had to help her.

The door to the mobile burst open to the sounds of heavy footsteps on the metal treads and the crackle of police radios.

"Come on," Swift cried, hauling them both to their feet. "We need to find Lily."

Annie felt a gentle tug at her ankle and looked down to see Mrs Haversham pulling at her trousers. Leaning down, Annie heard two words fall from her lips.

"Common room."

Swift shouted some instructions to the two officers and flung the door open. Annie followed as quickly as she could, nodding acknowledgement at Mrs Haversham, her ankle grinding beneath her with what must be a break or a fracture, or something else that meant bone was rubbing against bone. The pain was white hot, which was weird against the cold shivers wracking the rest of her body. The top of the metal steps felt like it could be the peak of Everest, but she bit her lip and grabbed a hold of the slippery railing, leaning over it so all her weight was through her upper body. If the worst came to the worst, she could slide down it, doubled over at her waist. And as a sharp jolt of pain shot up her leg, Annie decided that was the best way to get down them. It was only as she was manoeuvring her body to get a better angle, that she felt her feet lift from the floor.

"Apologies," Swift said, as he threw her over his shoulder like a fireman. "But needs' must."

He placed her gently on the mud and grabbed her left arm and threw it over his shoulder. Propped up, Annie found it easier to hop alongside Swift.

"Thank you," she said, finding her stride as they took the path back to the school building. "Do that again, though, and I'll kick you in the balls."

Swift snorted, hoiking her up a bit so he could step over a giant puddle of mud.

"Noted," he said.

They slid over the mud, the rain hammering down onto their heads. Annie's forehead had started to heat, and she knew she was running a temperature. But finding Lily was more important than how she was feeling. She grabbed Swift's collar and huffed out a breath as she saw the door to the Haversham's private residence come into view, the doorway illuminated still by the flickering light in the hallway and the torches of the searching police officers.

"We need to get to the common room," she shouted.

"Officers are doing a sweep of the school, they've searched the common room, but have come up empty handed," Swift said, his voice sounding strained with the added effort of keeping Annie upright. "The grounds and Levi's house have also given us nothing. What are we missing, Annie? Where has Florence taken Lily?"

They rounded the building and came to a stop at the door. Annie took her arm down from Swift's shoulders and leant against the cold stone, shivering and wet through. She pictured Florence, the young girl who had played herself so well as a victim. The way she had sat on the chair in the common room and spoken about her parents as though they were keeping her prisoner. The way she had played the victim all throughout her school life yet managed to come out on top. The wind whipped around the building and knocked Annie off balance as icy blasts of rain pummelled her face and neck. She reached up to pull her collar up when a jolt of a memory lit up in her head.

"Swift," she said, pushing herself up from the wall and landing on Swift's arm with a thud. "I have an idea."

Swift nodded, lifting her arm over his shoulders again and opening the door to the Haversham's private residence. Inside was warm and dry but Annie couldn't shake the numbness of the tips of her fingers and the end of her nose. Or the shivering that was still coursing through her body. Swift half carried her down the corridor, past the kitchen and the office to the internal door through to Foxton's.

"Nearly there, hang on." Swift said, as they made their way around the marble entrance hall to the other side of the stairs.

Flashing blue lights from the carpark outside made the hallway feel like a strobe lit rave. It made Annie's head swim and she squeezed her eyes tightly shut and put all her trust in Swift's strength to guide her to the cosy common room. She didn't have the strength to speak, her pain was getting worse. The sharp grinding in her ankle was now joined with a dull ache that thumped all the way up to her head. With her eyes shut and the warmth of Swift's body against her own, Annie felt like she could have a rest, just a small rest, a few minutes to let her body recuperate. It would be so easy to sit on the squashy sofa and shut her eyes for a little longer.

Shaking herself, Annie forced her eyes open. Too easily she had been taken a hold of by the numbing feeling of the pain in her leg. She couldn't get this far then stop. She owed it to Lily to at least try and help.

Swift pushed through the heavy door to the common room and slipped Annie's arm down from his shoulders again. He gave her his elbow and they both squeezed into the room. A warm glow from the last of the embers in the fireplace was welcoming and stopped some of Annie's shivering. She leant forward and grabbed the arm of the sofa, putting her weight through her arms and her good leg, she pivoted around and sat where she had sat a few days earlier listening to Florence's lies. The cushions sagged under her weight and Annie knew she would not be getting up from there in a hurry. She closed her eyes and tried to fine tune her other senses; touch, smell. She waited. Swift must have known she was on to something as he kept quiet, sitting himself down on the high-backed chair nearest the fire. He was as still as the air in the room and Annie couldn't hear him so she focussed back on herself, pulling her coat off and exposing as much skin as she could without succumbing to frostbite from the remaining soaking layers. The fire crackled and fizzed, the last of the embers trying their hardest to catch the oxygen and stay alight.

Then she felt it.

TWENTY-FIVE

ANNIE WAITED, HOLDING HER BREATH. THE ROOM cracked around her, impatiently.

There it was again.

A breeze, cold against her now bare neck, sent Annie's spine running with what felt like insects. Her eyes snapped open and Swift sat back in his chair, his own eyes fixed on her face.

"Did you feel that?" she said, and Swift shook his head back and forth.

The room flashed brightly with a bolt of lightning. With colours so vivid, Annie saw the picture of the decapitated head of John the Baptist.

That's it!

Florence had glanced at it more than once, and Annie had assumed it was because of its macabre nature, but maybe it was more than that. It was a huge painting, hung behind the sofa on the long wall between the door and the fireplace.

"The painting, Swift," Annie said, pushing herself up from the sofa with a huge amount of difficulty.

The pain that had lulled to a dull thudding shot up Annie's shins as though they were made of razor wire. She cried out in pain as her foot hit the floor, feeling bile rise up in her throat. Swift came to her, his arms outstretched to help her.

"No!" she cried. "Go. Go."

Swift looked between Annie and the painting behind the sofa, back and forth, back and forth. Instead, he ran to the door and hauled it open.

"Get an ambulance in here," he yelled. "Now!"

Annie was around the back of the sofa before Swift, she held a hand up to the painting, feeling around the edges.

"Look," she said, as Swift joined her. "Feel this."

She took his hand in hers and lifted it to the right-hand side of the painting, to the outstretched hand holding John's decapitated head by the hair.

"It's a breeze?" he said, his forehead wrinkled. "How?"

"I felt it back when we were talking to Florence in here," Annie said, starting to push at the artwork. "I shrugged it off then as my nerves about being in such an old building, but what if that's not it. What if the breeze is coming from somewhere?"

Swift started moving his hands around the other edge.

"God," Annie continued. "It's like it's been staring us in the face."

Swift slid his hand up and winced, pulling a bleeding forefinger to his lips.

"Ow," he said, sucking away the blood. "What do you mean?"

"Salome." Annie nodded at the painted woman with the less than innocent smile on her face. "Daughter of Herod the second. Original bad girl, asked for the head of a man who had opposed her mother's marriage on a plate and got it. Not one to argue with, I imagine."

"You think?" Swift was eye level with poor dead John's head.

"There's got to be a switch or something," Annie said, running her hands up and down the side. "How does the door to the Haversham's open?"

Another bolt of lightning bathed the room in bright white.

"I just pushed it," Swift said, standing back from the painting.

He took hold of the edges and pulled; the large piece of artwork fell towards him. They both stepped back, flinching, leaning on the back of the sofa. Annie bit her lip against the pain until she felt it pop between her teeth. The painting swung around, hinged on Annie's side, and revealed a dark passageway and a gust of freezing, musty air. It made the hairs rise up on the back of Annie's neck, something primal and instinctive screaming at her to stay in the common room. But she battled it and pushed off the sofa to follow Swift through the hole the painting had left. They stepped over the threshold into the dark, Swift flicked on his torch and the light bounced off years of cobwebs, thick with dust and hopefully not spiders. The floor was stone, uneven and slippery with dust, but the walls were close enough that Annie could brace her arms on either side. They crept along the corridor, silence filling her ears like glue. Not even the torrent of rain was loud enough to permeate through the walls. Down they went, the corridor sloping gently towards the underneath of the old school building. Annie wondered if they were heading to a disused cellar or an old cold room once used for storing meats over the summer months. The idea of meats hanging from hooks to be salted and preserved made Annie shudder, but still they pressed on.

Her heart was hammering through her chest with the added exertion of having to lift her body weight with her arms.

"What's that?" Swift stopped abruptly, holding an arm up. "Listen."

She listened into the silence, trying to hear past the sound of blood in her ears.

Rrrriiiip. Rrriiiiip. Rriiiip.

With his hand still raised, Swift motioned for them to move forwards. Annie felt fear pool in her stomach. Ice cold and dripping. The noise sounded like the scraping of furniture or the sharpening of a knife.

A door stood closed at the end of the corridor. It was narrow and short, a throwback to when the help was malnourished and able to squeeze through small spaces. Made of dull, cracked wood, tiny slivers of light poured through the gaps. Swift leant forwards and pressed an ear to the splintered wood. Annie listened from behind him. The noise was still there, regular, rhythmic.

Swift lifted a hand and counted down on his fingers. Five. Four. Three. Two. One. He grabbed the handle and turned, pushing the door open into a light so bright that Annie struggled to see what was going on.

"Shit," she heard Swift yell as she blinked away the spot in her eyes.

She felt herself gag with the stench. It was ammonia, she'd recognise that anywhere. Urine and the raw smell of fear. As her eyes became accustomed to the bare bulb, Annie swept them across the room. It was little more than a cavern, sloped ceilings built in brick to retain the cold, held up by thin brick pillars. Shackles hung off every wall between sconces that were recently used given the unlit candles that hung with dripped wax. Meat hooks dangled from the lower parts of the ceiling, polished and incongruously shiny amongst their surroundings.

Her eyes swept back, and the sight almost dropped Annie to her knees. The noise, the terrible ripping, became apparent. Florence stood like a mad woman at the far end of the room, her red hair was stuck around her face that had the sheen of the dead. In her hands was a rope, looped through the meat hook above her, squeaking over the metal as she pulled with all her might. The other end was noosed around the neck of Lily Parker. The missing girl swung limply like a doll, the floor under her was splattered with blood and what Annie thought must be urine given the smell that was still hitting the back of her throat with its acrid fingers.

"Florence," Swift shouted. "Let her go."

Florence looked at them with darting, wide eyes. Her

mouth stretching into a smile and she opened it and screamed.

"Noooooo!" It was almost inhuman, coming deep from within the young woman in a low rasp that made Annie's skin crawl.

Florence pulled at the rope with all her might as Swift ran right at her. Lily swung from her neck, back and forth, back and forth. She was giving up no struggle and her tongue was starting to push through her bluing lips.

"Annie," Swift yelled, nearing Florence. "Get her down."

Annie sprang into fight or flight mode, her ankle forgotten as she limped across the uneven stones to the dead girl. *No, she's not dead, she can't be.* As Annie reached Lily's body, Swift had almost made it to Florence. But the girl was quick. She twisted the end of the rope around one of the shackles on the wall and ran towards the back of the cavernous cellar.

"You all need to DIE!" she screamed, her words echoing around and bouncing off the ceilings. "You RUINED my life."

She held her hands out, the whites of her eyes gleaming in the darkened corner away from the swinging light bulb. She began to pace back and forth, spit flying from her mouth.

"You thought it was okay to talk about me? To spill my secrets?" She was yelling at Lily as Annie grabbed hold of the swinging girl's ankles and tried to take their weight. "No one can take LEVI away from me. NO ONE!"

"Swift," Annie yelled, ignoring the hatred flying from Florence. "Untie that rope."

Swift moved quickly, pulling the end of the rope free from the shackles and letting it drop gently so Lily fell into Annie's arms. The added weight buckled Annie's ankle and they both dropped to the floor. Working quickly, ignoring the searing pain now radiating from her leg, Annie flipped the dead weight of Lily onto her back and listened for a breath.

"Shit," Swift yelled, and Annie glanced up from Lily's chest to see him pacing. "She's vanished. Just disappeared and there's no bloody signal down here."

"She can't have just vanished into thin air, follow which way she went," Annie yelled back, watching Swift drop into the shadows of the cellar before turning her attention back to the prone body of Lily.

With Swift not here, the only light was from the swinging bare bulb above her head, the movement of light along with her pain was making Annie feel seasick. The walls swayed in and out and her vision dotted with tiny little stars.

"Stay with it," she yelled at herself now. "Stay with it."

Lily wasn't breathing. Annie had no idea how long she had been hanging by her neck or if she'd been drugged like the others, so she hauled herself to her knees and leant over Lily to start CPR. If there was a chance, even a slim chance, that Lily wasn't completely gone, Annie had to take it. She pressed down hard on Lily's chest with her clasped hands, feeling the ribs bounce under the heels of her palms. Thirty times Annie counted, before she leant down and breathed twice into Lily's mouth. Her lips felt cold and hard. Back to the chest compressions. Pounding as hard as she could, Annie felt her own strength sap out of her body. She had no idea if help was on its way, or even if they'd know where to find her. But she couldn't stop. She had to keep going until help arrived.

A scream echoed through the cellar. Bile rose in Annie's throat as the wail bounced off all of the walls and hit her ears, assaulting her from all angles.

"Get off me. You're going to regret this. You're all as bad as each other. You only care about yourself. No one cares. No one cares. NO. ONE. CARES."

It was Florence, there was no doubt about it. And as the crackle of the police radios arrived, and Swift shouted at Florence that she was under arrest, Annie felt a hand on her shoulder and turned to see the green uniform of a paramedic and her colleague standing over her. Then the walls fell in on her, the grey specks that had been dancing around the edges of her vision clouded it all as she finally gave in to the pain.

TWENTY-SIX

Annie saw the bright light and immediately panicked, struggling to sit up. She was too young to be dying. She didn't want to walk into the light, not yet, not when she'd just discovered a job she loved and a team she loved even more. Was Lily okay? Had she been in time to save her? There was the mystery of her missing sister, Annie couldn't go to the grave not knowing how she was and who she was now she was grown up. The phone call she hadn't made to her Mum. The cat she'd never owned. The children she'd never borne. The...

"Annie?"

The light moved and Annie saw the friendly face of the paramedic, a torch in his hand, and relief flooded her body. Closely followed by embarrassment.

"I'm fine," she said, swinging her legs around from the ambulance stretcher and trying to work out where she was.

A searing pain shot up her leg as she landed on the

gravel of the car park of Foxton's. Grabbing the side of the stretcher, Annie tried not to wince.

"Not so fast, young lady," the paramedic rushed around the bottom of the gurney and grabbed Annie's free elbow. "You're sporting a nasty displaced fracture of the medial malleolus, plus a dislocation. You're lucky you still have a pulse in that foot of yours or chances are we would have to amputate."

Annie didn't need to look down to see her cut away trousers flapping at her ankles, or her ankle itself three times the size it should be.

"Where's Swift?" she asked, panic rising in her as she hopped back around and pulled herself up to sit on the stretcher, her legs dangling over the edge. "Is Lily still alive?"

The paramedic's answer was cut short by an angry shout. Annie swung her head around to see what the commotion was and was greeted by the sight of Swift struggling to contain Florence despite the fact she was handcuffed and flanked by two huge, uniformed officers. A glob of spit flew past Swift's hair and landed with a thud on the gravel.

The car park was illuminated with spotlights, drag marks in the gravel where they'd been taken from the police van and set up to highlight the front of the school.

"Annie," Swift yelled. "Glad to see you're okay?"

He glanced down at her ankle and grimaced.

"Get off me!" Florence was angry. Her face was puce, wet with rain, her hair stuck to her as she thrashed to try and break free from her shackles. "They deserved what they got, stupid bitches. They were going to break my trust. Me? The one person who held this whole bloody school together. They would have been nobodies without me. How dare they?"

She was screaming like a banshee.

"It's over, Florence," Levi shouted over her rants, as he was walked by an officer down the steps of the school and to a waiting cruiser.

"Levi, love," Florence started crying, reverting back to victim in a heartbeat. "Tell them it's not my fault. I was pushed. They were going to tell on us, I know it, Emily had a secret and I had to stop her because it was about me, about *us*. If they told, then Dad would have had to stop our relationship, let you go from the school. I did it for you, Levi. We're worth more than them. We're so special." She stumbled a little over her own feet. "Oh, I don't feel well. They've got me too tightly, Levi. Help me."

Florence's eyes rolled back, revealing bloodshot whites as she shook her head. She looked possessed, but Annie knew it was all a trick. Florence was the master manipulator. Levi faltered on the gravel. After years of being told to look after her, he was as under her spell as her friends had been.

"Florence?" Levi walked tentatively towards her; his officer shouted but Swift held up a hand. "Flossie, listen."

She stopped struggling and gave Levi a sweet smile. Swift kept his hand aloft and the officers around Florence stopped too, they all stood, waiting to hear what Levi had to say.

"I knew you'd be bright enough to believe me," Florence said, quietly. "I thought scratching that proverb on Emily's arm would have been enough to keep the others quiet, but they were too stupid to understand, obviously."

"Emily's secret," Levi went on, shifting his weight between his feet. "It wasn't about us."

"Of course, it was." Florence burst out laughing, but Levi stood firm, shaking his head.

"It wasn't," he said. "Nothing at all to do with us, in fact. A few weeks ago, I... I saw her in the woods, and she was crying. So, I stopped and asked if she was okay."

Florence's face was turning, the smile slowly sliding away.

"Why were you talking to Emily alone?" Florence spat, then seemed to check herself. "Is that not against staff policy, I mean? You could get in trouble for being alone with a student out of hours."

Levi's eyes dropped; his whole body seemed to sag. "It wasn't after hours and it was in the school grounds, Florence. Anyway, this isn't the issue. The issue is that Emily thought she was pregnant. That was her secret. She just kind of blurted it out to me, as though she couldn't keep it contained any more. Then she begged me to forget what she'd said."

Levi ran his hands through his hair. Annie balked, *pregnant?* Had they missed this at the autopsy? Did the father of the baby know? Or had it been a mistake? Emily had thought she'd been pregnant, that's why she'd gone home to seek help from her mum and dad, that's why she'd been quiet with Dan Barker. Keeping her secret had eaten at her, yet it *was* a mistake and if she'd just had someone to look out for her, who could have helped her do a test or go to the doctor, then none of this would have happened. But Emily had been all alone, her friends had never known because Florence had been too worried about herself to care.

"I couldn't forget," Levi went on. "But I didn't say anything to anyone. I told her to talk to her friends about it, that maybe they... you could help. I wish I hadn't now. Maybe she'd still be alive. Maybe they'd all still be alive."

All? Annie felt tears prick her eyes. So Lily hadn't made it, she'd been too late.

"You should have told me," Florence said, her voice cold, her mouth a thin line. "It's all your fault, Levi. Why?"

Levi shook his head. "I have looked after you for so long, Florence. Kept an eye on you, tried to keep you out of trouble. Your mother used to, but then she started drinking instead, and it's having the same effect on me. I can't do this anymore. I thought you had started to change, but that's never going to happen."

He reached up and touched the cuts on his forehead.

The broken glass, Annie thought. It hadn't been Levi smashing things in a fit of rage in his cottage, it had been Florence.

"You're ruined," Florence yelled, her arms wriggling again to get free of the two officers. "Just you see, ruined. You're never going to work with children again. You're a paedophile. You're sick. No one will believe your testimony about me because all you ever do is lie."

She was really struggling now, the two officers braced their legs and lifted her off the ground screaming as they carried her safely to the waiting police van.

As they pushed her inside, Levi got as close as he could and tilted his chin up at her.

"You can't tell me who I am anymore," he said in not more than a whisper over the rain. "I'm free of you. I know who I am and it's not what you want me to be. You're nothing Florence, nothing but a bully."

And he turned and walked away, not flinching as she screeched obscenities at him, not looking up as he passed her father who looked like he could sleep for a thousand years. He just kept walking until he was through the throngs of police and disappeared into the darkness. Mr Haversham took one look at his daughter and sighed, climbing into the back of a marked police car with the assistance of a heavy browed officer.

Annie felt Swift's hand on hers before she saw him, engrossed as she was in what was unfolding in front of her.

"You okay?" he asked.

Annie nodded for a moment before changing her mind. "Not really," she said, wiping the tears from her face that were replaced just as quickly by rain.

Swift gathered her up in a hug and squeezed so tight the paramedic told him to ease up a bit.

"We did it, though," Swift said, sitting next to her on the stretcher. "Without you, we never would have found Florence, or Lily!"

"But it wasn't soon enough."

"Florence is going to be locked away where she can do no more damage. It wasn't enough to save Emily and Una but think of all the others you've helped. Florence wasn't going to be changing her ways. She's probably a certified psychopath."

Annie shuffled around so she could see Swift.

"Wait?" she said. "You didn't say Lily?"

"Lily is having her stomach pumped," he said, softly. "She'll take a long time to heal physically, there wasn't as much Rohypnol in her system as the other two, but it was enough to knock her out. But you saved her. The other paramedics said you were doing CPR, even with that foot, and you saved her."

He nodded down at her rapidly swelling ankle and Annie noticed it was turning blue. But her heart swelled at the thought Lily was okay. Physically anyway. Mentally she knew it would be a much longer road.

"And Hetty Haversham?" Annie felt sorry for Florence's mother. From what Levi had said, Florence had driven her to drink. How else could a parent cope with having a narcissistic psychopath for a child?

Swift nodded. "Lotta blood loss, but she's going to be okay. Apparently, she had seen Florence that night, watched her walk away from the woods with a bundle of letters that she'd promised to hand out and hadn't. Hetty Haversham took it upon herself to give those letters to Una and Lily to make Florence look less guilty for having one herself. Can you believe it?"

Annie felt her shoulders sag as Swift stood from the stretcher. It was over. *Almost.*

"What about Strickland?" she asked, a grin forming on her lips.

Swift laughed. "Not shown his face yet, I imagine

he's going to be keeping a low profile for a while amongst his non-swinger pals."

Annie chuckled and felt the last of the energy dissipate from her body. The paramedic lifted her legs up and swung her around, dropping a blue blanket over her before strapping her in.

"Let's get you to hospital," he said, wheeling the stretcher around to the back of the ambulance as the police van sped off down the driveway. "You'll probably need surgery. At least a six-week recovery time. Minimum."

He aimed the last word at Swift who raised an eyebrow.

"You're welcome to stay at mine if you can't navigate the stairs to your own place," Swift said, grimacing.

Annie's brain whirred with the mystery women's jacket in the back seat of his car, the dishevelled look, the times he'd not wanted to go home, and the weird smell of perfume he'd had stuck to him recently.

"No, you're okay," she said, smiling. "I'd hate to get in the way of your new lady friend!"

Swift's face flushed and he rubbed a hand down it, syphoning off the rain. His rumpled brow didn't stay rumpled for long. The penny must have dropped as another cheeky smile swept over his lips.

"My Mum, you mean?" he said, grinning. "She came to stay with me for a week too long. Nice to see you're paying attention to my love life though."

And he gave Annie a wink and headed off to his car.

THANK YOU!

Thank you so much for reading my book. It's hard for me to put into words how much I appreciate my readers. If you enjoyed Foxton Girls, please remember to leave a review. Reviews are crucial for an author's success and I would greatly appreciate it if you took the time to review Foxton Girls.

You can also find me here:

 facebook.com/ktgallowaybooks

 twitter.com/ktgallowaybooks

 bookbub.com/profile/k-t-galloway

ACKNOWLEDGMENTS

What a wonderful thing it has been to see Annie O'Malley and DI Joe Swift gain a following of readers who love them.

Thank you to everyone who has picked up a copy of FOXTON GIRLS after falling for the friendship and banter between Swift and O'Malley in CORN DOLLS. You're the reason I love writing.

Thanks also to Bev my wonderful editor, and Meg the fantastic cover designer! You both bring my words to life.

Thanks to Mum and Dad for reading and spotting bits I've missed. And to the rest of my family for encouraging me to keep going. You're all stars.

Printed in Great Britain
by Amazon

35132661R00131